Southern Sizzle

Part 1

Dedication

I dedicate this book to my mother, Katherine. She is the beat in my heart that keeps me alive and the voice of motivation that keeps me going.

Synopsis

Southern Sizzle captures the unwavering bond between first cousins, Saniyah Walker and Reese Dixon, as they navigate the triumphs, trials, loves and losses of early adulthood on the Mississippi Gulf Coast. Saniyah is an aspiring chef who experiences a whole new world of liberty, opportunity, and harsh reality when she leaves her hometown and the watchful eye of sheltering parents to pursue her dreams. Reese, Saniyah's roommate and life-long best friend, is a hotel receptionist who masks a deep fear of commitment with materialistic motives and sexually-uninhibited behavior until her internal struggle is put to the test by a triangle romance with life-altering consequences. On virtually opposite paths, Saniyah and Reese find themselves being pulled apart by men, ambition, and repercussion. But through highs of romance, success, and personal discovery and lows of betrayal, abuse, and self-destruction, the unconditional love they share keeps them together.

July

Chapter 1

As soon as Saniyah stepped out of her parents' two-story brick home, the heat engulfed her like a blanket. Being born and raised in Mobile, Alabama, she was used to the humidity, especially on a July morning, so she glided with ease through the thick air from one era of her life to the next. Although she didn't realize how much, Saniyah was about to embark on the journey that would change her life forever. She had never set foot outside of the state of Alabama, but she was gearing up for a one-hour ride to a new career and a new home in Gulfport, Mississippi. She wouldn't be far from the comforts of her hometown, but Saniyah knew she would be far enough to keep her parents and their opinions on how she should live her life at bay. She couldn't help imagining.

Saniyah was all smiles as she walked toward her parents, who were wearily packing a car with her belongings. Her long, wavy brown hair blew in the wind that was picking up, and her extra-large Nike T-shirt rippled off of her slender 5-foot-7 frame. The ballast in the gravel walkway crunched under her all-white Air Force Ones, and the old beat up, baggy blue jeans she only wore to clean up and do yard work flapped in the muggy breeze. Her green eyes, the ones that always caught the stares of others, gleamed as she took in the sight of her belongings being crammed into the black 2004 Honda Accord her mom and dad had just given her as a graduation present.

Just two months ago, Saniyah had graduated at the top of her class from the Alabama School of Culinary Arts. Even after her mother made excuse after excuse about why she should go to college instead, she stood her ground and got just what she wanted. She had always loved to cook. Even as a little girl, she would sit in the kitchen for hours watching her Grandma Rose cooking on Thanksgiving, Christmas, or just for the fun of it, she was attached. Her grandmother had taught Saniyah everything she knew about cooking and was the only one who encouraged her dream of becoming a chef. And as the wife of respected surgeon, Dr. William Walker Sr., she had also been a big help in providing connections and the funds that Saniyah's mother refused to waste on "silly cooking classes."

Although Grandma Rose died from breast cancer shortly after Saniyah started school, her granddaughter pushed herself to continue pursuing her dream in honor of her grandmother's honor. That passion reaped rewards as Saniyah impressed her teachers and peers with a keen sense of taste and presentation. Every dish she tried, from soul food to French cuisine, turned out brilliantly, and it wasn't long before her family took notice. Her success in school and the delicious taste of her cooking is what finally convinced her parents of her undeniable talent.

From that point on, they began to support her goals both mentally and financially. And their support turned out to be a very necessary investment because every restaurant in the Mobile area had turned down her applications. Each one offering the same excuse that they already had established chefs and didn't need any more help, inspiring Saniyah to try a new place with better opportunities.

"Ain't you gonna help us pack *your* things?" Saniyah's mother Alice asked. Saniyah snapped back to reality and looked into the green eyes that were responsible for her own.

"Yeah, Ma, just let me take this all in," Saniyah said. "I can't believe this day is finally here."

"Well, I still don't like it," Alice chimed in. "But I might hate it less if you got off your lazy butt and helped us." She wiped the sweat from her pasty, wrinkled brow and glanced over at her husband, Will, who was leaning against the car. He knew this conversation was not headed in a positive direction and was planning to take a short break while his wife and daughter exchanged the verbal blows.

"You still hung up on this Reese thing?" Saniyah asked her mother.

She was referring to her cousin Reese Dixon, who she was going to live with in Gulfport. Although her mother appreciated that her daughter and her niece shared a connection similar to her and her sister's relationship, she wasn't too fond of Reese and the way she lived her life. And she was definitely not excited about her only child sharing an apartment with the "rebel" of the family. She loved her niece, but the girl was trouble, and she did not want Saniyah getting caught up in Reese's drama.

"Baby, do you have to stay with her?" Alice pleaded. "Why don't you get your own place out there, or better yet, just drive over there from home every day? It's only an hour away."

Saniyah turned away from her mother's persuasive attack and dug her French manicured nails into her Coke bottle hips. Her mother had always been able to talk Saniyah out of doing anything she didn't agree with, except when it came to her cooking passion. So Saniyah was determined not to back down to her mother's demands.

"Ma, Reese is my best friend. Why wouldn't I want to stay with her?" Saniyah tried to explain.

"Why would you want to stay in a place with different men in and out all the time?" Alice snapped. Saniyah had opened up a debate Alice was more than prepared to win. "And you know she probably smokes that grass?"

Saniyah had to crack a smile at her mom's outdated vocabulary. She was well versed on her cousin's misbehavior and her mother's disdain for it. And though she would never let her mother know, Saniyah was looking forward to the possibility of adventure that a life with Reese would offer. It would definitely be more exciting than living the rest of her life in a house with a nosy mother and a laid back father who never took sides.

"It's weed, Ma." Saniyah corrected. "And Reese doesn't mess with that stuff…"

"Oh, that's right," Alice smirked, "Her boyfriends just sell it."

"Ma, stop it!" Saniyah reprimanded. "You don't know that."

"The hell I don't. Angie tells me everything that goes on with that one." Alice confirmed. "And you know if anybody knows the truth, it's Angie."

Her mother was referring to her just as nosy little sister and Reese's mom, Angela. Aunt Angie was known to let everyone in the family's dirty laundry, anyone who would ask, including her own and especially Reese's. It was almost like she got a kick out of baring her only child's imperfections to the world.

"Daddy, are there any more boxes in the house?" Saniyah changed her focus to her father, who was still enjoying his break. When he didn't answer, Saniyah knew he had slipped into one of his little daydreams he used to block her and her mother out during their arguments.

"Daddy!" Saniyah shouted.

"What, Baby girl?" He cried, annoyed that he had been startled out of his vision of money that would be rolling into his accounting firm during tax season. Soon the green dollar signs were replaced with his daughter's face. *"She looks so much like her mama."* He thought.

Will's observation was spot on. If his own coal black skin hadn't lent to Saniyah's slightly darker than white complexion, his Caucasian wife and half-and-half daughter would be mirror images stuck in different timeframes. He often wondered how two people who looked and acted so much alike could fight as much as his wife and daughter. But what he was sure of was that he was going to miss his little girl.

"Are there anymore boxes left?" Saniyah repeated.

"Nope. That's it, Baby girl." Will said, realizing his time protecting and caring for his little girl was growing thin. She was growing up, and although he knew it would come eventually, he somewhat regretted letting go of his only child. His eyes welled up, but he held back his emotion. The last thing his daughter needed was to be held back from her dreams. And though he had his reservations about it, he was determined to give her freedom to live her own life.

Alice, on the other hand, wanted to give keeping her child home one last shot, "Baby, do you have to go?"

Saniyah's heart fluttered at the sight of her mother's pleading pout, but the expression did nothing to deter her mission. She responded with a gentle kiss on mother's cheek and wiped off the smear of lip gloss she left behind. Her mother looked up at her and forced a smile. The pain of letting go almost made her cry, but she held her composure. Her mother's stare was firm, but the softness in her eyes let Saniyah know she finally had her blessing.

"I love you, Mama." Saniyah said.

"I love you too, Baby." Alice replied before releasing her embrace. As her hands fell to her sides, she realized this woman before her was not her baby anymore, and it was time to let her grow up.

Saniyah walked over to her father and took both of his hands in hers. They felt so soft and warm, with clean, manicured nails, truly the hands of a white-collar man. He gently pulled them from her grasp and placed them around her neck, pulling her forehead to his lips for a good-bye kiss. She threw her arms around him and he followed suit.

"I love you, Daddy." She whispered into her father's ear.

"I love you, Baby girl." Her father replied. "You be safe and take care of yourself."

"I will, and it's only an hour drive. I'll be back to visit." She assured her parents. With that, she got into her car and hit on the ignition button. She rolled down the window to say her final good-byes to her parents. She blew them both a kiss and smiled. As much as it seemed like the perfect time for her to get emotional, she was too excited about what was in her future to cry over her past. She would see her parents again, but it was time for her to live for Saniyah. And she knew she had to do it on her own.

Saniyah waved a final good-bye and sped down her parents gravel drive toward the open road of Interstate 10 and the opportunities ahead. Her parents, who were becoming a waving, yin-and-yang blur in her rearview mirror, held each other tight as the distance between them and their child grew wider. They held their pose and their view of her car through moist eyes until she was gone.

Will smiled, "Don't count on that visit happening anytime soon?"

Saniyah pulled into Gulf Villa Apartments around noon. She parked in front of Reese's downstairs apartment and looked up just in time to see a half-naked woman yelling up at a half-naked man on the top floor of the building. The woman had a dark-brown complexion and short black hair. She was attractive, but she didn't hold a candle to Saniyah. She was petite at about 5-foot-2, standing there in nothing but a lacy, red bra and panties. The man was a complete knockout. He was about 6-foot-4 with a dark brown complexion and a beautiful face, as far as Saniyah could see from the inside of her car. His body was trim, but he was exquisitely built. His rippling arms, chiseled legs and a perfect eight pack reminded Saniyah of the basketball players she was always crushing on in high school. But what she really couldn't keep her eyes off of were the gray, cotton briefs he was wearing that left little to the imagination.

Besides the fact that she was completely infatuated with this man she didn't even know, Saniyah couldn't help her curiosity. So she rolled her window down and listened.

The woman cried, "Baby, I'm sorry. I don't know what I was thinking about."

The man cut her off, yelling, "Whatever. I'm sick of your shit, Tisha. How the Hell you gonna call me some other dude's name?"

Tisha pleaded, "I'm sorry, Baby. You know I love you. It was an accident."

Tisha's man yelled back, "Shut up. If you loved me we wouldn't be out here making fools of ourselves in front of everybody. This the last time I'm gonna let you do this shit to me. I'm done!"

Tisha whined, "Andre, don't act like that.

He didn't mean nothing to me..." Andre cut her off again, "Well, you should've thought about that before you fucked him." Andre folded his arms and twisted his mouth into a sneer. "Now get up outta here 'fore I call the police."

Tisha's begging face turned stone cold. She snapped, "Well, fuck you then. That's why I fuck around 'cause you a little bitch that can't handle his business."

Tisha's words bounced off Andre like they were dipped in rubber. He was determined not to fly off the handle. The last time he was this mad at Tisha he busted out every window in her car with his bare hands, leaving him with several stitches in both hands. He looked down at his scarred hands and knew he wasn't going to let her get to him again, and he definitely wasn't taking her back.

"I'll be a bitch if that means I can get rid of your ass." Andre spat. "Now get the fuck away from my house, Trick."

"Who you calling a trick?" Tisha barked. She could barely get her words out before Andre darted back into his apartment. Saniyah thought this signaled an end to the confrontation and was preparing to exit her car until Andre came flying back outside with his hands full of clothes. Tisha realized it was her clothes he was holding and held up her hands, signaling for him to stop whatever he was about to do with them.

Andre yelled, "Here's your shit, Bitch. I'mma pack it for you."

Andre let the clothes fall out of his hands toward the ground. Blouses, dresses, jeans, jackets, and even a few pairs of shoes floated down to the pavement. Tisha ran to rescue her belongings, but she was too late. She picked up a red pair of stiletto heels, now freshly smudged with grease from the pavement, and suddenly caught an attitude to match.

Shaking one shoe in the air, Tisha replied, "No you didn't. This is Gucci. These shoes cost more than your whole damn life, Nigga. You gonna be sorry about this shit."

"Whatever." Andre shot back. He walked back into his apartment and slammed the door. Tisha gathered up her clothes and ran to her red '95 Toyota Corolla. She opened the door and shoved her disheveled belongings in the back seat. She jumped into the driver side and took off without hesitation. Saniyah could see Andre watching Tisha speed off from his apartment window. He stood there watching until she was no longer in sight. Then he abruptly closed his blinds.

Saniyah let out a nervous laugh and took a few seconds to regain her composure before exiting her car. But the other witnesses to the altercation seemed unfazed by the scene. *"They probably do this shit all the time."* Saniyah thought.

After a few more laughs, she headed toward Reese's place. She stopped in front of apartment 101, lifted a corner of the 'Welcome' mat off the concrete walkway, and retrieved the spare key from its hiding place. Reese had sent a text the night before to let her know she may not be home when Saniyah arrived. And a glance at the vacant, oil-stained gravel of Reese's assigned parking spot verified her absence.

Saniyah unlocked the door and walked over the threshold and into one of the most modern, sophisticated living rooms she had ever seen. Everything meshed perfectly, and everything was perfectly placed. White walls ran into clean, white carpet, and the windows had long, lacy black curtains. All of the furniture was black, including a 60" plasma screen TV that commanded the most attention. On top of the glass coffee table sat a huge black vase filled with freshly-picked white tulips, and even the picture frames were a mixture of black and white.

Saniyah was not expecting it, and the more she looked around the apartment, the better the décor became. She couldn't help wondering what Reese was doing with herself to keep up such a nice apartment. *"I know front desk clerks don't get paid enough for this."* She was definitely planning on getting to the bottom of that mystery.

With all the excitement of the day, the packing and the drive, Saniyah was feeling a little drained. She searched around the living room for the remote only to find there were four possible suspects. After turning on and off everything but the television, she picked the right one and sunk into the plush leather sofa.

Saniyah flipped for what seemed like an eternity when she spotted a picture of herself and Reese when they were kids sitting on an end table. She picked it up, and all her exhaustion was replaced with anticipation. God must have felt it, as well, because as soon as she picked up the picture, she heard the scratch of footsteps coming up the walkway followed by the sound of a key jiggling in the doorknob. The door swung open, and Reese was standing on the other side of the threshold holding a brown paper bag full of groceries.

Reese was fresher than Saniyah had ever seen her, rocking the short, Halle Berry cut, which was still perfect - an indication that she hadn't been out in the humid hairdo-killing air too long. Her 5-foot-4 curvy frame was draped in a pair of cuffed dark blue denim shorts and a tight-fitting white baby-T that barely reached her belly button. She completed her outfit with blue flip flops and a pair of black Christian Dior sunglasses that covered half of her face. Saniyah was impressed and then ashamed after looking down to examine her own raggedy appearance.

Reese, struggling to close the door with the bag in her hands, didn't even notice her cousin sitting on the couch until Saniyah sang their shared greeting, "What's the business, Cuz?"

Reese turned around so hard she almost dropped the grocery bag and had to catch it with her knee. She put the bag down with a cool smile hiding her excitement and walked toward Saniyah, who was smiling from ear to ear.

Without another word, the cousins locked each other in a hard, long-awaited embrace. Reese pulled Saniyah back to verify her presence was legit. She couldn't believe Saniyah finally made it to her neck of the woods. They almost never got to see each other, with the exception of an occasional family reunion, funeral, or wedding, and even then it was always Reese who was traveling to Alabama, the family homestead.

The two looked at each other, continuing to size each other up, seeing what had changed and what hadn't since they'd been apart. But aside from Reese's new haircut, not much had changed. It had only been a year since they were together at their cousin Clara's wedding. The thought of being together all the time sunk in, and the pair could no longer hold in their excitement. No longer constrained to an over-the-phone relationship, the novice adults began their childhood practice of jumping up and down with shouts of joy when they were in each other's presence.

When they calmed down, Reese picked up the grocery bag and took it into the kitchen, and Saniyah followed. They started putting away the items in the bag.

After the groceries were put away, Reese said, "Damn. We got so much to catch up on, huh?" She grabbed Saniyah by the hand and pulled her into the living room.

They sat on the couch as Reese brought Saniyah up to date about all of the men she had been with since the cousin's last deep conversation – a mere two weeks ago. She revealed the new men and those they had discussed in the past as the sponsors behind the beautiful appearance of her apartment.

According to Reese, her "victims" shelled out dollar after dollar to keep Reese from kicking them to the curb. But once their giving shrunk too low or their feelings grew too high, Reese called a wrap to their romance. Commitment and paying her own bills were concepts she had yet to consider.

Saniyah enjoyed hearing Reese go on and on about her crazy life, but she really wanted to ask Reese about the chef job she had lined up. So she let Reese continue on with her sugar daddy stories until she was out of them and then got straight to the point.

"So what's up with this job you got for me?"

"My friend, Ryan Taylor, wants you to work for him." Reese explained. "He owns a club called Humidity on the beach, and he's building a restaurant next door. He loved the food you sent over here and wants that kind of cooking for his place."

"Okay, so when do I get to meet him, interview, or something?" Saniyah asked anxiously.

"Chill out, Girl." Reese replied. "You'll meet him soon. And don't worry. I'm real cool with him so he won't put you through much."

This put Saniyah at ease, but she wondered what Reese meant by "real cool." She didn't want to get fired because Reese was no longer feeling her boss, but Reese reassured her without being asked.

"We used to mess around, but now we're just friends."

"What happened?"

"Girl, he told me to get my own hair done." Reese snapped. "You know I don't play that."

Both girls cracked a laugh, and Saniyah suddenly remembered the sexy dude from the parking lot. She was dying to find out more about him, and knowing Reese's gossipy ways - courtesy of Aunt Angie - she had to know something about the mystery man.

"Reese, who is that fine ass man who lives right above you?" Saniyah asked.

"You mean Dre?"

The name "Andre" was familiar to Saniyah from earlier, so she knew Reese was on the same page. She answered, "Yeah, that's him."

"When you saw him?" Reese asked.

Saniyah, anxious to tell what she knew, began blurting out the whole story of the parking-lot brawl while Reese listened closely, laughing along the way. After Saniyah finished, she wanted to ask Reese more about Andre, but she was interrupted by the sound of the doorbell. Reese's face filled with curiosity.

Saniyah sat back and watched as Reese walked toward the door and opened it up. To their surprise, Andre Sullivan was standing on the other side. The beautiful man Saniyah had spied from far away became the even more beautiful man up close. He stood before them fully clothed, sporting a plain white T-shirt, black baggy Girbaud jean shorts, white Air Force Ones and a black, fitted Atlanta Braves cap tilted to the right over his small, freshly-trimmed Afro.

"What's up, Dre?" Reese asked.

"Nothing much, Reesey." Andre replied with a smile that showed off his dimples. Saniyah coughed a little to draw some attention. Reese, noticing her plea, invited Andre in to introduce them. "Dre, that's my cousin, Saniyah, from

Alabama."

Andre looked at Saniyah, noticing her for the first time. He seemed confused at the sight of her and his stare sent her nerves into overdrive. *"Why is he looking at me like that?"* She thought, while brushing off her face to assure nothing was on it.

Her fears were relieved when Andre finally said, "Damn, Reesey, she looks just like you." Reese laughed and Saniyah smiled uncomfortably, still shook from the awkward moment.

Saniyah stood up and shook Andre's hand. His strong grip felt so good touching her soft skin she did not want to let go. Andre was stuck on the resemblance between the two women and was hoping neither one of them noticed the excitement they inspired below his belt. He was definitely feeling Reese and had been for a long time so the sight of her and a spitting-image cousin pushed play on his threesome fantasy button. He focused on the mission that was inspiring his visit to calm his lustful thoughts.

"We still gonna go to Humidity tonight?" Andre asked. "Ryan been bugging me to get you up in there all week. What's going on with *ya'll*?"

Reese quickly replied, "Ain't shit going on between me and Ryan so get it out your mind, Boo."

"Whatever." Andre doubted. He knew Reese and Ryan had been together for a while two years ago, but the last thing he wanted was for his home boy to be pushing back up on the girl he was feeling right when he was finally single and had worked up the courage to pursue her.

Reese changed the subject. "Saniyah, you wanna meet your future boss tonight?"

"Sounds good to me," Saniyah replied.

Reese looked at Andre and said, "There's the answer to your question."

"Anyway, what you got to eat up in here, Girl?" Andre asked, rubbing his stomach. "I'm hungry."

"What I look like, the grocery store?" Reese replied.

"Yep."

"Well, I ain't got nothing cooked, but if you ask nicely, Saniyah might hook you up."

Andre looked in Saniyah's direction, and she looked up at him with that uncertain smile she had been wearing the whole time he was there.

"That's right. You the chef, huh?" Andre asked.

"That's me." Replied anxiously.

Her thin frame lent to his thin faith in her

cooking ability, but he was willing to give it a try. After all the fuss Ryan had made about her cooking, he figured it couldn't be that bad.

Andre asked politely, "Would you mind cooking for us?"

Saniyah quickly replied, "I can hook something up."

She retreated to the kitchen in search of something edible. All Reese had brought home from the store was junk food, fruit and Hot Pockets. After a few minutes of searching, she found where Reese hid her real food. She took out a frozen package of T-bone steaks and some other ingredients and went to work while Reese and Andre watched TV and joked around in the living room. Because this was not her kitchen, Saniyah was short a few things, but she managed to pull off grilled sirloin steaks, parsley potatoes, cornbread, and a chef salad.

When she laid that plate in front of Andre, his lip almost hit the floor. He was stunned at how delicious the food looked, and that feeling was magnified when he finally took the first bite. He was in love - with the food - and he ate every last crumb. Reese, ever concerned about her perfect figure, left her plate kind of full. Saniyah didn't eat anything as usual. She hardly ever ate her own cooking. The delight on the faces of people enjoying her creations was filling enough for her.

When they finished eating, the girls retreated to their rooms to change while Andre waited in the living room. Reese returned about 30 minutes in a skin-tight black mini dress that curved around her busty chest and apple-shaped behind and came to an abrupt halt before turning into her glistening thick-built, toffee-colored legs. She finished off the ensemble with a pair of three-inch black open-toe stiletto heels.

Saniyah followed shortly after and was a totally different person from the one who drove in from Alabama. She wore a short, sleeveless tan dress that V-necked down to her chest and revealed a little cleavage. It was so tight that it clung to her body and showed every curve her father's African heritage had passed along. She tugged at the bottom of the dress to assure nothing was showing. Reese's style was definitely not her own, but the way her cousin's dress draped her body, Saniyah could not deny how good she looked.

Saniyah topped off her outfit with a pair of tan stiletto sandals, also courtesy of Reese. She wasn't used to wearing heels and it showed in her clumsy wobble. Her hair flowed down over her shoulders like water. Both girls had doused themselves in body glitter, perfume, and scented lotion that made the whole room smell clean and fresh.

Andre put on his hat and paused his threesome fantasy long enough to say, "Let's go, Ladies!"

Andre pulled his black 2006 Mustang into the parking lot of Club Humidity around 11:35 p.m. The party trio exited the car and headed for the door. The line to get in was winding around the building like a restless, impatient snake.

They walked to the entrance hand-in-hand. As they passed by, every person in the line gave them evil stares, their jealousy hissing faintly in the air. Lil Wayne's voice and the loud bass-filled beat of "Go DJ" were blasting from the sound system as soon as they walked through the entrance. There wasn't an empty spot or cup on the dance floor.

Instead of making their way to the floor, the trio made their way upstairs to the VIP section. There they were greeted with a complimentary bottle of Moet and a special booth to themselves. They didn't hesitate to crack the bottle open and inhale the luxurious intoxication.

As the three toasted to a good night, Ryan Taylor walked over. Club business had kept him busy all night. He was a bit tired, but when he saw familiar faces, it lightened his mood.

He walked over and called out, "What up people? Where the Hell y'all been?"

Ryan was not as tall as Andre, standing at about 5-foot-9. He had a yellow chalk complexion and a skinny frame. His hair was neatly braided into zigzag cornrows. He was not a muscle man like Andre, but the way his blue silk dress shirt hung on his body showed that he had a nice build. And his black slacks and matching black dress shoes were indications of his pretty-boy taste.

As he reached the table where the trio was sitting, his eyes were immediately drawn to the attractive new face with the beautiful green eyes. And he slid into the side of the booth right next to her.

Reese noticed his stare. "Ryan, this is my cousin, Saniyah, the chef."

"Stop lying, Reese. Don't no chef look this good." Ryan smiled, examining Saniyah's figure.

His comment amused Saniyah, and she let out a slight giggle. Her smile and beauty had Ryan enchanted, and the player in him was determined to have her.

"So you were the one that sent that delicious food over here, huh?" Ryan questioned. Saniyah looked at him and answered with a slight nod. She was not totally into Ryan. Although she found him attractive, he had a conqueror vibe about him, and the twinkle in his eyes told Saniyah she was his newest conquest.

Reese read Ryan's attraction, as well, and made it her mission to see that the two hooked up. Reese was determined to break Saniyah out of her timid shell, and she knew Ryan - with his sparkling personality, great taste and wealthy lifestyle - was the perfect man to do it. Reese was all too familiar with Ryan's scorecard, but she also knew that Saniyah was a smart girl and beautiful enough to expect more than a one-night stand.

"Andre, you wanna dance?" Reese asked.

"Yeah." Andre's leap in tone revealed the

excitement his cool disposition was trying to disguise.

The two got up and headed for the dance floor, leaving Saniyah and Ryan alone. Saniyah knew what Reese was doing. And although she felt slightly betrayed, she went along with it. Ryan was still catching glimpses of Saniyah's body. She tried to ignore the attention he was giving her, but when their eyes finally met, the sparkle in his auburn brown gaze intrigued her. She smiled and looked away nervously, but Ryan kept his eyes locked on her with a smile revealing his insanely white teeth.

"So, do *you* wanna dance?" Ryan asked.

"Sure."

The two made their way to the dance floor to join Reese and Andre. The deejay had just put on R. Kelly's *"Down Low."* All the couples in the crowd were hugged up and the single people were in hot pursuit of a partner to join the grind fest.

As they danced, Ryan asked, "So…did you leave your man in Alabama?"

Saniyah replied, "No. Actually, I'm single right now."

"Get outta here. I know you got somebody."

"I haven't had a boyfriend in about a year."

"What? Alabama dudes must be tripping passing up somebody like you."

"And what do you think makes me so special?"

"Shit….You fine as Hell, you seem like a nice girl, *and* you can cook. That's the total package right there."

Saniyah was surprised and flattered by Ryan's comments. He appeared to be so sincere in what he was saying and that attracted Saniyah to him a little more than she liked. She thought, *"Either I'm drunk, or this fool's game is tight."* She decided that it must be the alcohol getting to her. She couldn't believe Ryan could be into her that deep without an ulterior motive. Her mind was so concerned with what she thought were Ryan's possible plans that she barely noticed his hands moving slowly down her back.

When it occurred to her what he was doing, his hands were already in place, gently gripping her behind. Saniyah wanted to pull them back to their starting point, but his soft caress and memories of her year-long drought caused her to let it slide. She even took it a step further by laying her head on Ryan's shoulder.

Reese had been watching Saniyah and Ryan the entire time. She couldn't believe that Saniyah was actually letting him get that close so soon. She didn't know whether to break them up or let Saniyah do her thing. She was well aware of how satisfying a night with Ryan could be, but she also knew the makings of a one-nighter when she saw them. And a woman letting a man she just met grope her definitely fit that category.

Andre noticed Reese staring over at Ryan and Saniyah. He glanced over at them to see what was so eye-catching. He was just in time to see Ryan lean in and devour Saniyah's lips. The kiss caught him off guard, and he looked down to find Reese was just as stunned by the premature display of affection.

Reese cried out over the music, "What is she doing?"

"I don't know, but it looks like she's enjoying the Hell out of it." Andre laughed.

Reese's thoughts drifted to a vision of her favorite cousin crying on her shoulder and the sounds of her mother and aunt nagging her about letting Saniyah get caught up. She knew her Aunt Alice would talk Saniyah into going back home if she experienced any negativity in Gulfport. She thought, *"I can't let this go any further."*

Reese left Andre behind and began walking toward the love scene. Andre followed and grabbed her arm, yanking her back, just as she was about to tap Saniyah on the shoulder.

"What you doing?" Andre asked.

Reese pulled her arm out of his grasp and looked up at him with venom in her scowl. "Mind your business, Andre."

"Why you trying to mess up Ryan's

game?" Andre laughed.

"Because he's running his game on my cousin."

Reese turned away from Andre to continue her task only to find that Ryan and Saniyah were walking out of the front entrance. She knew Ryan had convinced Saniyah to go home with him.

"Damn, Andre, see what you did?" Reese cried.

"What *I* did? Andre didn't do shit." He snapped. "I don't see why you having such a fit anyway. I thought you *wanted* them to hook up."

Reese frantically explained, "All I wanted him to do was dance with her, maybe exchange numbers, not take her home and bang her out!"

Andre laughed, but the return of Reese's venomous glare let him know she was serious.

"Look, Reese, why don't you just calm

down and let your cousin do her thing?" Andre proposed. "She's a big girl. She can take care of herself."

Andre's words were making sense to Reese. Ryan hadn't forced Saniyah to kiss him, and he certainly wasn't taking her out of the door against her will. Reese thought, *"Who am I to stand in the way of her good time?"* She decided not to interfere and let Saniyah handle the situation.

"You're right."

"Of course I'm right." Andre boasted. "I'm *always* right."

"Whatever."

"So we leaving, or what?"

"We might as well." Reese huffed. "All the excitement just left out the front door."

When Reese and Andre got back to her place, they decided to have a few more drinks. They sat down on the couch, and Reese flipped through the channels on the television. Once she had found something worth watching, which happened to be a rerun of Good Times, they both cuddled close together. Reese suddenly remembered what Saniyah had told her about Andre and his girlfriend. Her curiosity was ignited.

"So….What was up with you and your girl causing a scene today?" Reese inquired.

Andre was a little caught off guard by Reese's question. He didn't think anybody he knew had seen his tantrum. But he was also aware that Reese was one of the nosiest people on Earth so he should've expected her to know something about it anyway.

"You all up in my business, ain't you?"

Andre snapped.

"Boy, save all the stalling and give up the details," Reese urged.

Andre knew if he didn't tell her, she would get the story from somebody else who most likely would not know what really happened.

Andre replied, "Alright, if you just gotta know, I found out she was cheating on me so I cut her lose."

"Damn." Reese whispered. "With who?"

Andre didn't want to revive the painful feelings about the breakup he had managed to suppress all night. "I don't know."

"Come on, Dre." Reese pushed. "Did you know him?"

"Look, Reese, I'm not trying to get into all that so can we just go back to watching TV?"

Reese could see that she had made Andre

uncomfortable. So she ended her investigation and pushed over toward him. She laid her head on Andre's shoulder, and he responded by putting his arm around her waist. Deep down he had real feelings for Reese, but after watching her drop countless men like flies - including his best friend Ryan - he was struggling with whether he should risk their friendship. It didn't seem like the best time, especially since he was fresh on the rebound. So instead of making a move that Reese seemed to be waiting for, Andre simply held her and continued to watch the television.

Andre smiled and whispered, "Forget the club. This is how you spend a weekend."

Reese laughed, "Watching Good Times with me?"

Andre gripped her hand and replied, "Good friends, Good Times."

Ryan pulled into the parking garage of his apartment building and eagerly jumped out of his like-new 2007 platinum E Class Mercedes-Benz. He ran around the front of the car and opened the door for Saniyah. She was amazed by how far she had let this night go, especially since she was with her new boss. She thought, *"Am I really going through with this?"*

Ryan took Saniyah by the hand and led her to an elevator door with an "Out of Order" sign hanging from it.

"Damn!" Ryan exclaimed. He led Saniyah to the stairwell and followed her up. His eyes were drawn to the sway of her hips. He thought, *"I'm gonna tear that ass up!"*

While they continued to climb to his second floor apartment, he mapped out his plan of attack. He wanted to give Saniyah his best performance. He had been with many women in his lifetime, but none of them were the thing of beauty walking in front of him. He was thinking farther than just a one-night stand for a change. He wanted to be able to say that lovely creature belonged to him. But he did not want a commitment, just the access to hit it when he felt like it and the confidence that no other man had the same luxury.

When they reached the second floor, Ryan directed Saniyah to his door. He anxiously pulled the keys out of his pocket and unlocked the door. His apartment was far from typical. Everything was coordinated and clean. The windows had beautiful curtains and blinds that complimented the furniture. The dining room table had four full place settings, tall white candles, and a glass cake dish that actually had a pound cake in it. There wasn't a video game console or joystick in sight. A fish tank full of exotic-looking fish sat in one corner of the room, and a 52-inch flat screen TV hooked up to a full entertainment system was at the center of the living room.

The appearance of his house made Saniyah even more uncomfortable. She thought, *"He probably has women up in here all the time."* She wanted to tell Ryan to take her home, but she could not fight the attraction she was forming for him. Great taste blended with good looks was a solid recipe for her surrender.

Ryan went over to the bar in his dining room and came back with two full glasses of champagne. He handed one to Saniyah, and they made a silent toast before taking a few sips. Ryan took Saniyah's glass and sat it down. He grabbed her hand and led her to his brown suede couch.

They sat down, and Ryan looked into Saniyah's eyes with an intense stare. Saniyah's nerves vibrated through her body, and she looked away from his piercing eyes.

Ryan gently grasped Saniyah's chin and turned her face back toward him. He leaned in and kissed her just as intensely as he was staring. He slowly put his hands up her dress and around her hips. But when Ryan began to pull at her panties, she gently pushed him away.

"What's wrong?" Ryan asked.

"I don't think I wanna go there, at least not tonight."

After all the work he had put in, Ryan could not believe Saniyah was not ready. But her attitude was one with which he was very familiar. He usually would have detected it early, but his instinct was clouded by his unusually strong attraction to

Saniyah. He also assumed she was a freak like her cousin, Reese, who was more than willing to sleep with him on their first night together. He thought, *"Damn...guess it don't run in the family."*

"So, what do we do now?" Ryan shrugged. "You want me to take you home?"

"It's kind of late," Saniyah said after peeping 3:30 on the wall clock above the television. "I'll just sleep on the couch....if you don't mind."

"That's fine with me, Sweetheart." Ryan's shoulders perked as he realized the opportunity in getting what he wanted out of the situation.

"I'm sorry about this, Ryan." Saniyah explained. "But I hardly know you enough to be sleeping with you already. The fact that you're my boss doesn't help either. I don't want to complicate that relationship."

"I understand." Ryan lied and his shoulders fell back into their disappointed slump. "I'm not trying to push you to do anything you don't want to do."

Saniyah was surprised at Ryan's consideration. His understanding attitude was fueling her growing attraction. She finally admitted to herself that he was someone she could see herself being with, but she wanted to take it slow.

Ryan gave Saniyah an old New Orleans Saints jersey to sleep in and showed her the way to the bathroom. She was changed within a few minutes and made her way back into the living room where Ryan was waiting on the couch with a blanket and a pillow. He had changed into a pair of blue silk boxers and a matching silk robe. Saniyah couldn't help but stare at his slim, defined torso through the opening in his robe, and she noticed him staring at her just as hard.

Ryan kissed Saniyah on the forehead and headed straight to his room. He finished what the vision of Saniyah's long legs stemming from his jersey had started behind a locked door. Saniyah snuggled into the blanket and closed her eyes. But they burst open when she realized the fate that awaited her when she returned to Reese's apartment.

"Damn." She whispered. "Gotta take the walk of shame and didn't even get none."

Chapter 2

Reese awoke to Andre's sleeping face resting on her shoulder. She smiled as she thought about what it would be like waking up to that sight every morning. But her fantasy was short lived. She had never desired a guy without knowing for sure that he was totally into her. And the way Andre had ignored the sexual intentions of her couch cuddle the night before had her questioning whether the attraction was mutual. She had always assumed his lack of desire for her sprouted from his commitment to whomever he was dating at the time. But his status as a newly single man knocked the legs off of that theory. Her own sudden craving for her best male friend was just as hard for Reese to decipher. She didn't know whether it was the break up or if her body was tired of denying what she really wanted out of their relationship.

Reese's brain froze with confusion. She closed her eyes and grimaced in deep contemplation until her mind wrapped around a conclusion she could deal with. It had been about three weeks since she blessed her last "victim" for his impromptu purchase of a diamond tennis bracelet she had yet to wear. So she thought, *"Girl, you just need some."*

Reese laughed and lifted herself out of the situation as the tension in her head eased back into equilibrium. She went to her room to change out of the club dress that was still clinging to her curves and put on a pink pair of Nike gym shorts and a plain white tank top. The bitter after taste of champagne was still on her tongue so she made her way to the bathroom to brush her teeth.

As her stomach started to rumble with hunger, Reese decided to wake up Saniyah and convince her to make a quick breakfast. But she realized, half way to Saniyah's bedroom, she didn't know if Saniyah was in there or not. Memories of the previous night started to come back. She said a silent prayer Saniyah had not gone too far with Ryan. But when she walked into the room, she discovered a made bed. She giggled and thought, *"That little hoe!"*

Reese turned to leave and her eyes met with Andre's chest. She gasped and jumped back in shock causing Andre to erupt with laughter. Reese smiled, slightly embarrassed by her reaction, and pushed him away. He stumbled until his back met the wall.

"You play too much." Reese wore a fake frown.

"But you like it, huh?" Andre smiled and reached out to tickle her.

"Stop, Dre!" She tried not to laugh and fought off his hands. She freed herself from his tickle trap and began to walk back into the kitchen. But Andre gently pulled her arm back.

"What are you doing?" Reese faked aggravation.

"Come here." Andre confidently ordered with an enchanting stare Reese had never seen in his eyes.

Andre pulled her close and wrapped his arms around her waist. Reese did not know how else to react so she did the same.

The intensity of his stare made her nervous. She started to question further, but he put his index finger over her mouth then leaned in closer until their lips met. They tasted each other for the first time, and Andre's right hand slid slowly down Reese's back and gripped her behind.

When their kiss ended, Andre stared down at Reese and was pleased to find her in a passion-infused stupor. He had mulled over whether he was going to make a move on her all through the previous night. And Reese's face told him he had made the right choice in going through with it. He just hoped she wanted the same kind of relationship he wanted.

"What the Hell was that?" Reese panted.

She leaned against the door frame of Saniyah's room to relieve the drain and let the world come back into focus. Andre leaned back against the wall and folded his arms. He smiled as he looked into her eyes, revealing two cute little dimples in his cheeks that Reese had never noticed.

"That was me letting you know I don't wanna be your friend no more." The sincerity in Andre's words sent a tingle up Reese's spine. She shivered, contemplating whether his advances were coincidence or a sign from God telling her not to ignore her feelings.

"How long you been feeling that way about me?"

"Since I've known you."

Reese was amazed. She could not believe he had hidden his attraction to her so well for their entire friendship. They had met two years earlier during a party at Ryan's apartment. At the time, Reese and Ryan were together. She was well aware of Andre's appeal, but she was not the one to cause drama between best friends. So she and Andre had developed a strictly platonic, sibling-like bond.

Reese suppressed memories of their first encounter and came back to reality. She wanted to tell Andre that she shared his feelings. But that time around, it would be the friendship *she* had built with him that would be in jeopardy if they took their relationship to another level.

Her longest relationship to that date was with Ryan, and that only lasted for two months. It took them a long, awkward six months to salvage their friendship after the break up. And their relationship was never as strong as it had been before they hooked up. Reese did not want this to happen with Andre. He had become like the brother she never had, and after growing up a lonely only child, she cherished their friendship. Losing him would be like losing a part of her family, and she knew that would be the outcome if a relationship with him played out like all those in her past.

"If you don't want to be with me, just be real about it." Andre broke the awkward silence floating between them.

"It's not that." Reese explained. "I just need time to think."

"I understand." Andre pouted with disappointment.

Guilt welled up in Reese's conscience as she examined Andre's pained expression. The rejection in his posture was something she could not recall ever witnessing from her usually happy-go-lucky, immaturely playful friend. It dawned on her how deep his feelings for her must have been, especially after being suppressed for two years.

Her brain freeze returned, but it was short lived as enlightenment followed close behind. She realized she could potentially be spoiling her first opportunity at real love with one of the most gorgeous men she had ever seen because of infidelity she did not even know if she would commit. So without any further thought, she declared to herself, *"Aww, what the Hell?"*

Andre did not know what to make of the confusion written all across Reese's face, but his body began to slump in defeat with every second of uncertain silence. Not wanting to face the rejection it seemed he was headed toward, he started to retreat to the living room. His experiences with the female sex over the past few days had been rough, and the emotion of it was starting to weigh heavy on his mind. He felt his rebounding impulse may have spooked Reese and ruined any chance he would ever have with her, not to mention the possibility of making their friendship awkward and artificial.

"Hold up, Dre." Reese called before Andre had the opportunity to create space between them. Andre turned to face her, and she pulled his face down into a fiery kiss. She pulled her lips away, after what seemed like an eternal lip lock, but the two held their embrace and passionate gaze.

"Okay?" Andre could not find the truth in all the mixed signals Reese was sending. But Reese's next statement made her feelings absolutely clear.

"I don't wanna be your friend either."

Reese put her arms around Andre's neck and pulled him down until their lips met once again. He wrapped her legs around his waist without breaking their kiss and carried her into the living room. He laid her down on the sofa and softly pecked her lips. Reese closed her eyes and braced herself. Andre kissed down her neck and chest toward her breasts. He slipped his hands under her tank top and felt her up until he found the clasp on her bra.

Just as Andre was about to unhook the tricky snaps, Saniyah walked through the front door. She screamed as soon as she saw them, but immediately covered her eyes.

"Oh my God!" She gasped. "I'm sorry!"

Andre jumped off of the couch and Reese shot straight up to a sitting position. Saniyah lowered her hands from her face and opened her eyes with caution. She smiled after noticing the uncomfortable dispositions of the interrupted lovers. Reese's embarrassment was written all over her blush red cheeks and nail-biting mouth, and Andre's neck scratching and darting eyes revealed his search for a believable lie. Saniyah put her hands on her hips demanding an explanation with her accusing eyes.

"We were just uh....playing." Reese stuttered.

"Playing, my ass! Playing what…hide and go get busy?" Saniyah laughed.

Realizing the ridiculousness of her impulsive statement, Reese joined in on her cousin's laughter. Andre chimed in with an uncomfortable chuckle before they all quieted down. The moment of silence allowed Reese time to remember that Saniyah was just getting in.

"Never mind us. What kept *you* so busy last night that you couldn't come home, Missy?"

"Why you all up in my business?"

Saniyah knew she would have to fill Reese in about her night at Ryan's, but she definitely did not want to do it in front of his best friend. She did not know Andre that well but reasoned that anyone who hung out with Reese had to be as big a gossip as she was.

"Because you my cousin and I was worried about you."

"Your ass didn't look too worried just a few minutes ago." Saniyah snapped.

"But we ain't talking about me no more." Reese shut down Saniyah's attempt to change the subject. "Now, be for real and tell me what happened."

Saniyah, sensing Reese had no intention of backing down, walked over to her and whispered into her ear, "I ain't saying a damn thing in front of him."

"Fair enough." Reese agreed. "Tell me later."

She decided to respect Saniyah's request because she *did* know Andre and understood that his strong bond with Ryan would not allow him to keep anything Saniyah had to say about his best friend a secret.

"Don't be whispering." Andre butted into their privacy. "Did my boy hit it or not?"

He was accustomed to only hearing sex stories from his home boys and was intrigued by the possibility of hearing a woman's perspective on the subject.

"This is family business, and *you* are not family so keep out." Reese's venomous words brought an abrupt halt to Andre's attempt to pry. He sat down on the couch with a defeated pout.

Saniyah was pleased by Reese's protective comment and flashed her cousin an appreciative smile before starting for her room. She wanted to take a shower and relieve herself of the unclean feeling she had about the events of the previous night. But as soon as she got to her bedroom threshold, Reese's voice stopped her progress.

"Saniyah!"

"What?"

"We hungry!"

"I'll cook when I get out the shower." Saniyah sighed. She didn't really feel like cooking, but she was not about to refuse any request from the person who was providing her with free room and board. She went into her room and closed the door behind her before sprawling out on the bed. Thoughts of her overwhelming first night in Gulfport filled her head until she ran her fingers through her disheveled hair and remembered she needed to freshen up. She reluctantly lifted off of her soft comforter and gathered her things before heading to the bathroom for a long, hot shower.

She stood in front of the mirror and smiled at the vision of her morning glow beaming back. Fantasies of the endless possibilities her journey might hold filled her mind. But they also made her realize how long her journey to success could take. She whispered to her reflection with uncertain anticipation in her tone, "One day down…who *knows* how many to go."

Reese and Andre sat in the living room with a fairly an uncomfortable silence. Neither of them knew whether to get dressed and save their little rendezvous for another time or try it again. Andre decided to make the first move and rubbed Reese's hand. She looked at him with a devilish grin that inspired him to grab her arm and lead their escape to her room.

After ensuring the door was securely locked, Andre embraced Reese from behind. He kissed her neck as he removed her tank top and tossed it on the floor. He put his hands on her stomach and examined the lines of her slightly toned abs before sliding his touch up to her chest. His slow, gentle touch was a welcomed break from the hasty pawing of Reese's past lovers. It occurred to her that he was not just in it for the penetration. He wanted to please her.

Andre led Reese to the foot of her bed. She fell on her back and waited for his next move. He continued his exploration of her body with a trail of kisses from her neck down to her Garden of Eden. Reese covered her face with both hands disabling her sight to enhance the feel of his touch. Andre licked a ring around her belly button with his tongue. Then he pulled at her pink, lace thong with his teeth. His playful nature amused Reese and she let out a tiny giggle. He began to pull more aggressively, and the closer he came to removing her panties, the louder she laughed. Her heart raced with anticipation until a knock on the door brought the passion to a screeching halt.

"Stop raping each other and come eat." Saniyah cracked a smile on the other side of the bedroom door then walked away. Reese's paradise faded away and Andre stomped into the bathroom, his manhood falling with each step. Reese sucked her teeth as she pulled herself up from the bed to redress.

"I'm gonna kill your cousin, Reesey." Andre paced back and forth with both hands on his head. He balled his fists in a boxing stance that rivaled Fred Sanford's and then plopped down on the edge of the tub with pouting lips. Reese laughed and put on her robe. She patted Andre's matted afro and then left him alone in the bathroom as she headed to the kitchen. Andre stood up from his seated position and looked in the mirror in disbelief. He pondered, *"Is her ass really worth all this waiting?"*

Andre peeked out into the hallway just in time to see Reese's figure glide into the kitchen. His appreciation for curves sent his gaze plunging down to her perfectly-shaped hips and thighs. He grinned and whispered, "Hell yeah."

Reese walked into the kitchen and was met with the breathtaking smell of Saniyah's breakfast feast. But her mind was far from focused on food. Andre was still lagging behind in the bathroom so Reese seized the opportunity to overwhelm her cousin with a private investigation.

"So you gonna tell me what happened last night?" Reese pried. Saniyah looked up from the stove and smirked. She saw no need to leave one fire to face another so she spoke her response over the morning delicacies simmering below.

"Hadn't planned on it." Saniyah's smile beamed with the pleasure of driving her gossip-hound relative mad with her evasiveness.

"C'mon, Niyah." Reese whined. "You gotta tell me something."

"Oh alright." Saniyah gave in, and Reese rushed to her side.

Just as Saniyah was about to air out her slightly stained laundry, her thoughts were distracted by the song and dance of her cell phone against her thigh.

"I'll tell you after this call." Saniyah deceptively promised. She pulled out her phone and silently laughed at the rejected scowl on Reese's face before greeting the caller. She slipped into the living room, away from Reese's eavesdropping ears.

"Hey, Sweetheart." The voice on the other end replied. Saniyah almost dropped the phone at the sound of Ryan's voice.

"Hey, Ryan. How you doing?"

"I'm doing fine now that I hear your voice again."

Saniyah chuckled, half flattered, half amused at Ryan's tired line. But she was happy he had made the effort to call her. She didn't want to admit it, but the smooth, enticing tone of his voice had her slipping into a fantasy of what could have happened the previous night.

"So when do I get to see your beautiful face again, Sweetheart?" Ryan's question brought her back to reality. "I've been thinking about you all morning."

"*Another line?*" Saniyah thought. Ryan's insistence to stick to his player script was annoying the attraction out of her. She decided to change the subject to avoid his advances.

"Why don't we discuss the menu?"

"What menu?"

"For your restaurant."

"Oh, *that* menu." Ryan laughed as his mind and tone shifted from pleasure to business. "Yeah, I guess we better take care of that. The contractors said they'll be done in about a month, maybe sooner, and I want to open up right away."

"When do you want to start planning?"

"We can meet tonight at my place if that's cool with you." Ryan's toned remained all business, but his mind was back to pleasure. Recognizing his intent, Saniyah made up an excuse.

"Tonight's not good for me. Reese is taking me to the Pass to visit family." She needed more time to figure out how to deal with his advances so she continued her lie.

"In fact, I'll probably be busy all this week unpacking and getting myself together. Maybe we can get together next week."

"How about next Friday?"

"Sounds good." Saniyah reluctantly agreed, knowing the meeting would eventually have to happen.

"Then it's a date."

Andre and Reese snuggled on the love seat in the living room and rekindled their flame with soft kisses. Saniyah managed to slip away avoid further questioning after her phone call with the excuse of a morning run, but Reese was more than willing to postpone her investigation for some alone time in the arms of her new pursuer. The yearning pair played it safe with innocent pecks and caresses, not wanting their fun to be spoiled by a third interruption. But the fire growing between them with every touch was too much to endure.

Reese leaned in and softly bit Andre's bottom lip before engaging in a passionate kiss. She put her arms around his neck and moved her lips from a kiss up into a nibble on his right ear. She moved down to his neck and slowly made her way back to his mouth.

After two failed attempts, Andre unsnapped her bra under her tank top. He moved his hands toward her breasts and started to caress them gently. Her moan excited him, evidenced by the poke of his pants under her thigh.

Reese's bra and tank top were frantically removed and flung down to the floor one by one, followed by the stretched out T-shirt, practically ripped from Andre chest. The feel of cotton against his skin was replaced by the soft, warm collision with her C-cups.

Reese released Andre from the constraints of his jeans and briefs and he leaned back so that she could guide him in. She cried out as they made contact and sunk her manicured claws into his back. She bit into his shoulder to muffle her screams.

Andre let Reese control the tempo. Her slow grind built to a mildly accelerated stroke, motivated by his light, impulsive slaps to both of her thighs until it was more like a raging bounce. The new pace brought Andre closer to his peak. He tried to hold on until Reese cried out.

"Ooh, Daddy!"

Andre could no longer repress his release so he filled her with his gushing explosion until his body tensed in climax. He holed out toward the ceiling like a scalded dog and squeezed Reese's thighs with both hands. His passionate ending curled her toes, and she clung to him as if her life depended on his support.

When the tension passed, Andre placed a single, exhausted kiss on Reese's forehead, and she collapsed into his snuggling arms. They held their embrace silently a few minutes longer before Andre lifted Reese from the couch. She wrapped her legs around his waist and her arms around his neck. He planted another soft kiss on her lips before transporting them both to her room. He laid her body down and climbed into the bed next to her. He pulled her into him from behind and held her tight. The pair laid there in blissful silence while the thick, lingering humidity from their passion lulled them.

As Andre started to lose control over his heavy eyelids, he kissed Reese's shoulder and peeked around to see that her lights were already out. Hoping she was not too far gone, he whispered into her ear.

"Well worth the wait, Baby."

August

Chapter 3

The week passed by quickly as summer slipped from the hot days of July into the blazing days of August. Saniyah spent most of her time unpacking and deciding on what recipes she wanted to use in Ryan's restaurant. She was having a hard time choosing the direction for the menu. But by the time Friday came around, she had narrowed it down to either a taste-driven soul food menu or a presentation-driven upscale menu.

She had been having second thoughts about meeting with to make the final decision. She even thought about calling and canceling because she did not feel ready to put up with his hot pursuit. It took every muscle and nerve in her being to pick up the phone and dial Ryan's number to confirm their "date."

Ryan's smooth tone filled the receiver, and Saniyah's body tensed. But she relaxed when she realized it was merely a recording on his voicemail. Her lips curled into a smile as she began to leave her message:

"What up, Ryan? This is Saniyah. I was just calling to...uh...confirm our business dinner tonight. So…uh....call me when you get a chance and let me know what the deal is. Look forward to seeing you. Bye." She quickly hung up the phone, took a deep breath and went back over the content of her message.

"*Look forward to seeing you? That's right, Saniyah, just give this dog the go ahead to sniff up your skirt all night.*" Saniyah lectured herself, but the mental reprimand came to an abrupt halt when visions of Ryan's bright smile and gorgeous eyes filled her mind. Her focus shifted from ambition to passion. She laughed at her crumbling resistance and thought.

"Hell, maybe I need a little sniff in my life."

Reese sat relaxed in a bubble-filled tub. Burning aromatherapy candles engulfed the room with tranquility, and thoughts of Andre entered her peaceful mind. She had made it through an entire week of total devotion, with not so much as a glance at another guy. But the thought of all the new sexual adventures and possible lucrative opportunities she was missing troubled her mind. Maintaining the balance between staying faithful to her new man and staying truthful to herself was becoming more of a struggle with every loyal day. She winced as the dueling desires wreaked havoc in her brain and thought.

"These aromatherapy candles ain't shit."

Reese laid her head back and tried to change the focus of her mind. She pictured Andre's cute, dimpled face and smiled with closed eyes. Thoughts of the banging sex they shared entered her mind and her hands drifted into the water and between her thighs.

Just as her massaging hands were about to become Andre's, the screeching ringtone of her cell phone pierced her ears and brought her out of her trance. She hesitated to move, but the phone's persistence made her jump out of her soothing soak, wrap a towel around her dripping skin and scurry to retrieve the phone from the nightstand beside her bed.

"Hello." She panted.

"What up, baby?" A voice Reese didn't recognize came through the receiver.

"Who is this?"

"Oh, damn. You done forgot me already?" The voice questioned, its tone becoming more apparent with each word. She smiled and hid her recognition, stringing her caller along.

"Hey…Darren. You know I couldn't forget about you, Baby."

"I got your Darren, Girl!" Andre's bark was playful but insecure.

"Calm down." Reese demanded. "I'm just playing with you."

"Well, I know your testosterone detector ain't disabled yet." Andre laughed with more certainty. "You only been off the market for a week."

"Ha, ha, ha." Reese snipped. "What you think I am…a sex addict or something?"

"No comment…"

"Anyway…what you call me for?"

" Just wanted to hear your voice."

"*Aww*, that's so sweet."

"I know…" Andre was about to continue his self-praise, but an authoritative voice called from the background.

"Gotta go, Boo. I'll see you tonight."

Reese hung up with a satisfied grin on her face. The aromatherapy was not able to ease her mind, but Andre's thoughtful call had done the job. The short, sweet conversation had reassured her faith in being faithful so she made up her mind to stay on the commitment wagon.

Finally at peace with her situation, Reese proceeded to get dressed. She glanced at the clock. It was 11:00 a.m., and her shift started at noon. She had just started working as the front desk manager at the Oasis Hotel three weeks before and was still trying to make a good impression on management.

She did not want to be late so she began a frantic race to get there on time. She pulled on her starch pressed uniform, combed out her recently bumped curls and bolted outside to her 2003 canary yellow Forerunner. Stop lights along the way would provide enough time to touch up her make up.

Once in her vehicle, Reese looked into her visor mirror to analyze what needed to be done to glamorize her already-flawless face. Her reflection had a new glow she hadn't noticed before. She smiled and admired the appealing vision from all angles before boasting.

"Commitment looks good on you, Girl."

Chapter 4

Ryan was busy turning his playpen into a love den Saturday night. Dealing with his club and contractors had kept him and his mind so occupied the meeting with Saniyah had slipped his mind until he checked his voicemail earlier that morning. He returned her call right away and apologized over and over for standing her up. She reluctantly accepted his apology, but her annoyance was apparent in her tone so he quickly rescheduled their meeting for that night.

With a new meeting set and his Saturday agenda cleared, he was frantically preparing his place for a potential rendezvous with his captivating colleague. He had cleaned every inch of his apartment before shifting his focus to ambience. He lit candles with scents named after passionate expressions, dimmed the lights to a faint glow, put on some mellow baby-making music, and set his flat screen to a scene of a blazing, crackling fire place, lacking only in its ability to imitate the warmth of its flames.

The doorbell rang just as Ryan was pouring two glasses of champagne. He was wearing a Navy blue and white-striped Polo shirt tucked into a pair of khaki Polo pants with Navy blue suede Timberland boots. Around his neck was a platinum chain with a diamond-studded cross hanging just below his heart. He made his way to the door and opened it without questioning the visitor's identity. To his surprise, Saniyah was wearing a pink baby tee with a white "S" in the middle, some white flare slacks and a pair of pink and white New Balances, a far cry from the sexy outfit he was anticipating. But he didn't let her appearance break his concentration.

"Hey, Beautiful. Come on in."

Saniyah walked slowly into the dark room, clutching her recipes in a portfolio at her side. She halted to take in the love scene she had walked into.

"So, we planning a menu or making babies?" Saniyah inquired.

"What?" Ryan replied.

"I'm just saying, you got all these candles lit and music going like you trying to get something started."

"Well, what if I was?"

"I'd have to shoot you down cause I came here to work." Saniyah's rejection was an insult to her true desires, but she did not want to seem too eager and dash any chance they had to be professional.

"Damn, Girl, why you gotta be so mean?"

"I'm just letting you know what's up."

Ryan did not want to risk making Saniyah uncomfortable by pressing the issue so he changed the subject.

"You want something to drink?"

Without waiting for her to respond, he made his way to the bar separating his kitchen and living room to retrieve the two chilled glasses of champagne he had already prepared. Saniyah was about to deny his offer, but refrained knowing the alcohol would calm her nerves. She sat down on the cozy couch, sank into its plush material and crossed her legs.

By the time she was settled in, Ryan came back and handed her a glass. She sat it down on the end table beside her as soon as it reached her hand. Ryan took notice of her actions as he sat down.

"You not gonna toast with me?"

Saniyah picked up her drink, knocked it into his outstretched glass, took a sip and sat it back down without any thought or attention for her host. She ignored the laser beams Ryan was aiming at her face and shifted her focus to her portfolio.

"So you ready to get started?" Saniyah pressed, her attention still firmly aimed at the portfolio in her lap.

Ryan cracked an astonished smirk and sung.

"Wow."

Saniyah picked up on his wounded tone and flashed a sweet, innocent smile in an effort to not seem totally inconsiderate of his hospitality.

Ryan shook his head in disbelief and laughed.

"You are something else."

Ryan lowered his lids and analyzed Saniyah with desire in his expression. Her impenetrable act intrigued him. He pondered whether the challenge she was presenting was sincere. And he was prepared to do whatever to find out. He lifted his lustful gaze to her smiling face and licked his lips as if he were staring at his favorite meal. Saniyah's eyes fell to his mouth and remained dazed before realizing her mistake and snatching her face away in shame.

"Are we gonna get started or what?" She hissed with frustration aimed more at her own slip up than at the wasted time.

"Show me what you got." Ryan purred in the velvet tone he used once it was apparent that a victim was falling prey to his seduction.

His tone flowed slow and sweet like honey through Saniyah's ears. She continued to look away knowing the sound and sight of his pursuit would only make her crave his touch, smell, and taste. She flipped through her portfolio. The words and images of her life's passion calmed her desire for physical passion. So she shifted their encounter to its original purpose.

"Well I was thinking about..." She started to present her ideas, but Ryan leaped from the couch and started swaying from side to side.

"Ooh, I like this song."

Usher and Monica's version of "Slow Jam" was streaming from the stereo system in perfect time for Ryan to redirect the situation in his favor.

"You like this song?"

"Yeah. I like it."

"You wanna dance?" Ryan said, holding his hands out to Saniyah to join him.

"Say what?" Saniyah ignored his pleading hands and folded her arms with an annoyed expression on her face. "I didn't come here to dance."

"Come on." Ryan said pulling Saniyah off of the couch. "Dance with me."

He began to playfully dance, swinging her arms as he moved from side to side. His antics brought a smile to Saniyah's face and weakened her focus. They joked around for a few minutes before Ryan pulled Saniyah close to him and held her tight. His grin fell back into a seductive squint as he peered down into her anxious eyes with admiration. He leaned in and their lips met for the second time. The tenderness of his kiss and the soft tickle of his freshly-trimmed beard against her chin stirred up the cream between her thighs.

Saniyah knew there was no turning back at that point. So she put her arms around him and submitted to the trail of kisses he left along her neck. His hands moved down to her legs and lifted them around his waist.

They moved from the living room to the hallway. Ryan pressed Saniyah's back against the wall and continued to tease her neck with kisses as he let her feet return to the floor.

"You sure you ready for this?" He whispered.

Saniyah moaned out something that sounded like, "Uh huh."

He began to unbutton her pants. She didn't resist or pull away so he snatched them and her panties down simultaneously.

"You got protection, right?" Saniyah pressed.

Although he had plenty in his bathroom medicine cabinet, thoughts of a condom were far from Ryan's mind. He continued to taste Saniyah's perfumed skin until he looked up into her questioning eyes looking back down at him.

"Don't move."

Ryan flew to the bathroom across from where they were standing. He tore open the medicine cabinet and grabbed his emergency stash of Trojans. A single hand and a strong rip from his teeth was all it took to get the baby blocker out of its package. Saniyah watched his every move with a photographer's eye. Before she could blink, his soldier was dressed and ready to march.

Ryan lifted Saniyah's legs back around his waist and achieved penetration. He began to move in and out, speeding up with each stroke. Saniyah hugged his neck tight. Moans and groans of pleasure seeped out of her mouth with his every move.

"You like that?" Ryan panted.

Saniyah's only reply was another moan.

After what seemed like a lifetime, Ryan's body began to tingle and the pressure of his approaching climax built strength. He began to pound harder and harder into Saniyah's body as if he was trying to nail her to the wall. The loud sound of banging picture frames and vibrating dry wall rang through the whole apartment. Saniyah's soft moans became loud pleas for mercy. She pulled Ryan's head down into her chest and let out an orgasmic howl. Ryan let his juices flow.

After letting the paralyzing tingle fade away, he and Saniyah slid down to the floor. They leaned into each other's bodies to rest their own.

Ryan mustered enough strength to speak.

"Ready to work?"

Saniyah came home to find Reese passed out on the couch in a red bathrobe and Winnie the Pooh slippers. She tried to sneak by her sleeping cousin. But just as Reese had been roused many nights in her childhood by the sound of her dad coming home from the "late shift," she was stirred by her cousin's subtle footsteps.

"So how was it?" Reese asked through her drowsy stupor. She sat up on the couch, wiping the sleep out of her eyes. Her words bounced off the back of Saniyah's neck halting her attempt at an escape.

"Excuse me?" Saniyah turned to face her slouching cousin.

"Don't play dumb, Niyah. You coming home at eight in the morning with your hair a mess and your clothes all wrinkled. I know that ain't happen making menu suggestions."

Saniyah looked down at her disheveled outfit and felt her tossed around hair. She tried unsuccessfully to straighten herself out.

"Bama girls need love too." Saniyah nonchalantly surrendered and slumped down beside Reese.

"So, how was it?" Reese repeated with a triumphant grin.

"Girl, there are no words!"

Reese cracked up with laughter.

"That good, huh?"

"My standards for sexual performance just quadrupled!"

Reese laughed.

"I see my boy still putting in work."

Saniyah froze.

"What are you saying?"

"I'm saying Ryan knows how to put it down."

"You had sex with Ryan?"

"We did date for a few months." Reese's tone wreaked of confusion. "I told you that. Didn't I?"

Saniyah flipped through her Rolodex of memories and came across Reese's vague comment about her and Ryan "messing around," but the word "date" was never mentioned. The butterflies in her stomach from the night before turned into flesh-eating tapeworms feasting on her insides.

Reese noticed the sick look on Saniyah's face. "Girl, what's wrong with you?"

"You never told me y'all dated."

"That was two years ago. We just cool now."

"By 'cool' do you mean y'all still get it popping every now and then?"

"Me and him are old news." Reese shrugged with indifference. "You can have him."

Saniyah winced.

"I can have him?"

Reese felt the annoyance in Saniyah's voice.

"You mad?"

"Hell yeah!" Saniyah's voice rose to an enraged tone neither she nor Reese could remember ever coming out of her mouth. "You got me over here all sprung on a dude you used to fuck on the regular!"

Reese leaned away from her cousin and raised her eyebrows in amazement.

"Hold up! Why you getting all fired up at me? I told you we were together." Reese raised her voice with more power and credibility than her newly volatile relative. "Whether we got down once or a million times, what difference does it make? It's over!"

"Well…"

"If anybody should be mad, it should be me." Reese rested her hands on her hips and pursed her accusing lips. "You went after my sloppy seconds without even asking me if I'm cool with it!"

Reese regretted saying the words as soon as they left her lips.

"*Wow*! You think that's what I was trying to do?" Saniyah spoke with astonishment in her tone with her hands over her insulted heart. "Maybe I would've asked for your blessing if I'd known you was dating him!"

Reese's fire was extinguished by the hurt in Saniyah's expression.

"Look, Niyah, let's stop this before it turns ugly. You my cousin, and I love you. I apologize for not telling you more details about me and Ryan. I just figured it wasn't necessary. If you really like him, don't let me ruin it."

Reese's words sank in and quieted Saniyah's inner rage.

"I'm sorry for blowing up at you."

"Friends?" Reese formed a pouting, pleading smirk and extended her arms.

Saniyah snuggled into the warmth of her cousin's arms and whispered.

"Always."

Chapter 5

Reese sat at the front desk of the Oasis Hotel watching the second hand tick on the large round clock above the front entrance. The empty lobby was quiet. She didn't know how she would make it through the next six hours. Counting seconds was getting old fast, and she had already memorized the words to the advertisement that continually played on the lobby's wall-mounted plasma TVs.

Reese was just about to go against company policy and send Andre a freaky text message when a tall, caramel-skinned brother came through the front entrance and walked up to her desk. The gorgeous stranger was built with perfection. Reese looked into his sparkling grey eyes and felt like she had been lost in them for days. His short curly hair was barely visible underneath his slightly tilted all-black New York Yankees fitted cap. His smooth, muscular arms rippled out of his short sleeves. His tight black T-shirt gripped his chiseled frame as if it had been glued on. His diamond-studded belt buckle peaked out over the edge of his shirt, holding up his loose-fitting charcoal jeans. And the diamonds in his belt were nothing compared to the binged-out platinum Rolex hanging loosely from his left wrist.

When the handsome stranger finally spoke, Reese was ready to give him whatever he wanted.

"Hi." He said.

His baritone voice sang through her ears, making her a little moister than she was comfortable with. She struggled to gain her composure and conjured thoughts of betrayal she would be committing to dash her desire to seduce the beautiful stranger. She searched her mind for a plan to keep the desires suppressed, but all she came up with was her rude-girl routine she usually used on unattractive guests who came on to her. Without much time to give it more thought, she turned on her ghetto attitude.

"I'll be with you in a second." Reese snapped. She looked down at the bubbles screensaver on her monitor, pretending she was doing something important. The stranger waited patiently for her to finish with a smile on his face, showing off his perfectly straight, glistening white teeth.

"Welcome to the Oasis. Can I help you?" Reese said when she felt he had waited long enough.

"I don't know. Can you?" His smile widened and Reese moistened.

"Do you need a room or not, Sir?"

"Does the room come with a date with you?"

Reese looked into the magnificent stranger's face with a concealing scowl.

"Sir, we do not provide that kind of service here at the Oasis. If you'd like, I can refer you to another establishment more suitable to your needs because this isn't the one."

"My bad, Sweetheart. I was just playing. You don't have to get all gutter on me." He pleaded. "I'm Terrence Forrest. I used to play ball at USM. Now, I play for the Cowboys."

His name didn't ring any bells with Reese, and she knew nothing about sports besides the fact that both Chris Paul and Reggie Bush could get it. She kept her act up and looked apathetically into his dreamy eyes.

"You know…*football*? Dallas Cowboys?" Terrence pleaded for recognition.

"*And*?" Reese snapped.

Terrance saw that his status as a local celebrity and second-string running back on "America's favorite team" was not going to be enough to impress the panties off. So he cut his resume-dropping short and got back to business.

"I have a reservation under Forrest."

"Finally, you get to the point."

While Reese checked on his room, Terrence continued to stare at her, and his eyes drifted to admire the buttermilk mounds that were peeking out from her half-unbuttoned blouse before returning his gaze to her super-model face. He was really blown away by her exotic beauty and curvaceous feistiness. Most of the clerks he encountered at upscale hotels were pale, average-looking white women wearing fake smiles and cheery attitudes.

Reese tried to ignore his stare and concentrate. But every time she looked up at Terrence, he flashed that praise-worthy smile. She tried not to make heavy eye contact with him to avoid his engaging eyes. So many thoughts were running through her head that after a few minutes, she hadn't found his reservation. She thought.

"Andre is your man. Do your job and stop thinking about this sexy, grey-eyed devil in front of you!"

With that thought, Reese finally buckled down and found Mr. Forrest's reservation.

"Here it is…fifth floor…room 522." She stepped away to retrieve his key. When she came back, he was still smiling at her.

"Hey, I'm sorry if I offended you earlier." He said. "I just wanted to get to know you."

"That's okay, Sir." Reese cracked a customer service smile. "Here's your key and enjoy your stay."

She quickly handed him his key before he had a chance to go any further with his apology. Terrence noticed her hastiness and was about to accept it as a sign of her disinterest. But he gave her one last smile as he took the key into his hands.

Reese looked into his eyes and froze. An unintentional smile forced her lips apart, revealing her own praise-worthy pearly whites. Terrence turned away without another word and proceeded toward the elevator with a bounce in his step.

When he arrived in front of the elevator doors, he looked back over his shoulder once more to find that Reese was still staring at him. She broke her daze and tried to focus on something else. She prayed silently.

"Lord, please give me strength!"

Terrance turned back to face the elevators and chuckled to himself before pushing the up arrow. He thought.

"She wants me."

Although Reese had confirmed her lack of interest in Ryan during their confrontation, Saniyah was still pondering Ryan's feelings for her. She needed to hear from his own mouth that he wasn't feeling her cousin before she could even think about getting any closer to him.

She called him up around noon after careful consideration of how she would handle his response – whatever it may be. After seeing Saniyah's name on the caller id, Ryan picked up and answered with his smooth, mellow tone expecting a sweet conversation.

"What you doing calling me, Girl?" He teased. Saniyah was in no mood to play so she got right to the point.

"Why didn't you tell me you dated my cousin?"

"What?"

Ryan was panic-stricken and loss for words. He had not even thought to tell Saniyah about Reese since he had only dated her for a few months. But he knew he should have at least mentioned having a sexual relationship with her first cousin.

"And the sex was good now that I think about it. Guess that does run in the family." He thought with a smile. A vision of the two cousins pleasing him at the same time filled his mind. His soldier hardened a bit before Saniyah's faint cough

over the receiver brought him back into their conversation.

"You talking about Reese?" He faked an unaware response.

"You fucking with all my cousins now?" Saniyah snapped. "Of course, I'm talking about Reese!"

Ryan laughed nervously taking in the seriousness in Saniyah's tone. He looked toward the ceiling, praying God would send him the right words to ease her mind and release him from her clutches.

"Baby, that was a long time ago."

"So what? You could've told me before I got involved with you!" She yelled. "Maybe I don't wanna share Reese's *sloppy seconds*!"

"*Sloppy Seconds*?" Ryan repeated in shock. He thought.

"How she gonna disrespect me like that?"

"Yeah. I said sloppy seconds."

"Look. Me and Reese only dated for two stinking? ass months." Irritation swelled in Ryan's tone. "Yeah. I had sex with her, but to tell the truth, there really wasn't a connection between us."

Ryan checked his aggravation and replaced it with self-pity, "I didn't even want to have to think about that time in my life again."

"Why not?" Saniyah wasn't buying it. "You didn't wanna remember to tell me so you could get in my pants quicker?"

"Oh my God. I can't believe you." Ryan said. "Here I am about to bare my soul to you, and you jumping all up on my case."

"Well, what do you expect?" Saniyah started. "Hold up....What you mean 'bare your soul'?"

A victorious grin graced Ryan's face as he took command of the confrontation between himself and his gullible opponent.

"I *mean* that your cousin really broke my heart."

Saniyah's coldness faded. She had forgotten that she was talking about Reese, the girl who couldn't commit if her life depended on it. She heard the pain in Ryan's voice and realized she may have reopened some unhealed wounds. Ryan continued with his lovesick exaggeration knowing Saniyah was falling for every word.

"Me and Reese were best friends and then I started having feelings for her. Next thing I know, we in a relationship."

"Go on."

"Well, I thought I really liked Reese, and I thought she felt the same way. But she didn't. She dumped me for some dope boy from New Orleans."

"Ricky?" Saniyah asked. She knew exactly who Ryan was talking about. Reese made Ricky a household name to Saniyah in past conversations.

"Yeah, that was the guy."

"So she hurt you, huh?"

"Felt like a slap in the face. That was the first real heartbreak I ever had. That shit hit me hard, especially since it was one of my good friends doing it to me." Ryan sighed, choking back fake tears.

"So, do you still have feelings for her?"

Ryan paused to ponder that question before replying.

"The only woman I'm feeling is you, Boo."

"Oh, really?" Saniyah's tone was sarcastic.

"Yes, really." Ryan's confirmation was music to Saniyah's ears, but she wanted to reiterate her displeasure with the way things played out so he understood her preferences in the dynamics of their future relationship.

"Well, I'm sorry that she hurt you, but you still could have told me."

"I know, Boo. And I apologize for not being honest with you. I will from now on because I see this thing between us going somewhere."

Saniyah didn't like his use of the word "thing," but the rest of his apology assured her they were on the same page. But in Ryan's mind, this couldn't be farther from the truth. His words were spewing, but there was a blockage in the sincerity behind them. He knew he would have to play the boyfriend role with Saniyah to keep her around.

And since the sex was on point, that's exactly what he intended to do.

"So you gonna be Ryan's girl, or what?"

"Are you gonna be Saniyah's man?"

"I think I can handle that."

October

Chapter 6

After two months of preparation, the Boiling Point was finally ready to open its doors to the world on a cool October night. A few days after their first argument, Saniyah and Ryan decided to buckle down and get the menu and other important things done before their deadline came too close.

The traditional soul food menu was set the tone for the down home theme. The interior decorators managed to create the illusion of being inside an old, country kitchen. There was a huge redbrick fireplace as the centerpiece of the back wall with an old, black iron stove next to it and a rack of old pots and pans hanging above it. The tables were made from weather-beaten wood and had white lace table cloths across the tops. A lantern served as the lower lighting for each table, and hanging down from above were several antique black and gold ceiling fans.

The grand opening was an amazing sight. The place was packed with the who's who on the Gulf Coast. For those who came without celebrity status or a reservation, it would be a long night of waiting in line. Neither Ryan, nor any of his staff had expected the huge turnout. But they were prepared enough to handle it.

The surge of people kept Saniyah on her feet all night without a dull moment. Her tired body was beginning to turn on her, but she fought through the sting in her heels and the stiffness in her lower back to make the night a success. The guests were raving about her cooking the whole night, and she had to make dozens of trips to different tables to be smothered with compliments like the white gravy on the biscuits she served with her southern fried chicken and cat fish.

Reese and Andre, who were to Reese's surprise still going strong, showed up and were given the VIP treatment. They were escorted to one of the best tables in the house with the best lighting and the clearest view of the star-spangled Gulf.

The hostess alerted Ryan to his closest friends' presence, and he quickly made his way over to greet and gloat.

"What's up, Y'all?" Ryan's voice belted out of his huge smile. "Did your boy hook you up or what?

He stood back with folded arms waiting to be showered with praise.

"Oh yeah. You did the damn thing, Man." Andre said extending his hand. Ryan gripped it tight and pulled his best friend up into a manly embrace. After that he pulled Reese from the table and bear-hugged her, too. Reese and Andre were stunned by the sudden display of affection, but their surprise went unnoticed. Ryan just smiled from one awestruck face to the other, poking out his chest and wearing his pride like Superman's S.

"I'm sorry." Ryan apologized for his aggressiveness. "I'm just so damn happy tonight."

"I bet you are." Andre agreed. "But why don't you get back to your thing and let us get some of Saniyah's good food before y'all run out?"

"Ain't nobody gonna run outta nothing." Ryan was confident, but Andre's comment had put him on alert to check inventory at his nearest convenience.

"Speaking of Saniyah…" Reese remembered. "Where the Hell is she?"

"She's around here somewhere…so busy, she can't keep still." Ryan explained. "But, anyway, I'm gonna let y'all get your grub on. Peace!"

With his two fingers raised, Ryan walked off into the mix of diners and servers and was not seen again by Reese or Andre the entire night. They briefly exchanged words with Saniyah, raving about her food, but before they could get their compliments all the way out, she had to excuse herself to handle a burnt-gravy situation.

"Man, I want something like this one day." Andre stated. "The casino gig ain't breaking this kind of bread."

He had always envied Ryan's success and money, and seeing the restaurant becoming a success on another level was motivating him to want to move on to something bigger and better for himself. He didn't want to live on a blackjack dealer salary forever. Thoughts of his dwindling funds soured his mood. And his bitterness showed in the slump in his back.

"Your day will come, Baby." Reese reassured. "And when it does, it'll be ten times better than this place."

Her words soothed her man's acidic frame of mind. She was making lemonade out of his lemons, and it was the best he had ever tasted.

"You right, Boo." Andre said with his cheerful mood restored. "I just need to let it ride."

"That's what I wanna hear." Reese cheered. "Now, no more talk about this sad-ass shit. You are going to be great in whatever you do because you are a great person. But forget all that success stuff right now and just have some fun. Please…for me."

Reese gripped Andre's hands and pleaded, batting her doe eyes that no man could resist.

"No more sad talk."

Andre was still stunned that Reese was hanging in on the relationship long enough to be supportive. He thought she'd be scoping some other man by then, leaving him at home curled up, soaking his pillow and blasting break-up songs. The last two months had been one of the most pleasurable times in his life. Not only did she give him some of the best sex he could stand, but she could also appreciate and respect him. Two things none of his past girlfriends ever did.

His train of thought gave him the urge to express something to Reese that he had never expressed to any woman outside his family. He gently clutched her left hand. With all the excitement of the restaurant, she barely noticed his touch, but he knew the next words out of his mouth would grab her full attention.

"You know I love you, right?"

Reese gazed at her own confused face in the bathroom mirror. She had played Andre's comments off by giving him a firm hug, a kiss and a compassionate "I feel the same way" look. Never once responding, she excused herself from the table and swiftly escaped to the ladies' room. Her first instinct was to go back out and tell Andre he was moving too fast. She wanted to be with him, but she didn't want to be pressured into expressing false feelings. She thought.

"Man, here we go again. Why do I always do this shit? Why can't I be in love for once? What is my problem?"

A vision of her father entered her mind. He had cheated on Reese's mother countless times, with numerous women, while she was growing up. Rumors by the mouths of gossiping relatives became evidenced by the estranged younger brothers Reese had only seen in pictures. Even at that moment, her father was still a relationship jumper, going from woman to woman without so much as a thought. And his fear of commitment had been inherited by his young and impressionable daughter -- the only female in his life he ever truly loved.

The vision of her father's time worn face returned to a more youthful, feminine version as she stared at her own reflection in the mirror. She did not want to continue following in his footsteps, but she knew she could not look Andre in the face and lie about her feelings. If he brought up the love thing again, which she knew he would, she would just tell him the truth.

Reese walked to the door and was about to reach for the handle when it flung open and two older privileged-looking White women walked into the restroom. They were both in their early 40's and were in mid-conversation when Reese's presence silenced them. She stepped back to allow them entry. One of the women noticed Reese's disturbed expression. Before Reese could make a move, the woman gently patted her arm. When Reese turned to acknowledge it, the woman's face was filled with compassion and Reese could tell she was going to pry.

"What's wrong, Honey?" The older woman inquired. "You look like you just lost your best friend?"

Ryan was still on cloud nine about the success of the night, and he knew he owed most of it to his leading lady. Saniyah had been one of the biggest factors in making this dream a reality. Without her food and creativity, his bustling restaurant would still be a quiet, empty space.

His attachment to her was growing a little more than he had anticipated. Earlier that week, he had actually thought about putting a picture of her on his nightstand. Love was not yet an issue, but the more time he spent with her, the more he desired to be in her presence. He was not yet disciplined enough to fully commit because he had been with several women behind her back. But none of those women had intrigued him the way she did. So he knew the feelings he had for her were different.

Ryan wanted to test the waters of their relationship and was brewing a plan to do so when he spotted his main dish slumping over the bar with her head resting over folded arms. He walked over to where she was sitting and gently tapped her on the shoulder. She turned around with a grimace of exhaustion, expecting another staff member requesting assistance.

"Damn!" Ryan blurted. "What's wrong, Baby? You tired?"

"Hell yeah I'm tired!" Saniyah grunted. "I've been on my feet all night."

Ryan tenderly brushed Saniyah's hair out of her face, and began to massage her shoulders. He worked magic on her muscles, and she could feel her tension loosening.

Ryan saw their rare alone time as an opportunity to share his feelings with Saniyah and give her a much-needed break. As he continued to work the kinks out of her neck, he whispered.

"I need to ask you something so let's go in my office."

When they got into his office, Ryan began to pace the floor back and forth. This made Saniyah very nervous. She thought Ryan just wanted to fool around for a minute, and she was prepared to pull the "I'm too tired" card. But the seriousness on his face let her know something else was on his mind. He pulled her closer to him and took both of her hands in his. He gazed into her eyes, his own darting from corner to corner.

Ryan's analyzing expression relaxed to compassion as he revealed his question.

"Why don't you move in with me?"

"Come again."

"You heard me."

"Boy, don't play." She smiled.

"I'm serious."

Saniyah searched his eyes and found truth in them. The weight of the decision he had laid upon her was heavy, and there was a lot more than a relationship riding on it. So she took a seat at his desk to mull over her options.

The silence was killing Ryan. He didn't want her to think about it. He wanted a "yes" and refused to accept any other answer. Ever the salesman, he decided to speed things up by presenting her with the perks of having him as a housemate.

"Think of how close we could be if we lived together." He pitched. "We could find out whether or not we're meant to be together. It's a great way to test our relationship."

"I know, but that's a big step, Baby. I need to think about that for a while. Give me a few days."

"I can't wait that long. I need an answer now." Ryan pressed. He knew the only way to break Saniyah was through words of loyalty and adoration. He kneeled down in front of Saniyah and gripped her thighs.

"Do you know that you stay on my mind whole day, every day?" Ryan admitted. Realizing how much his statement sounded like a player line, he tried again.

"I mean that. I'm not just saying it to get you to say yes. You are the one person in this world that I truly care about and want to be around all the time. At first, I thought we were just gonna have fun together. But now, it's like I can't make it through the day if I don't see or talk to you."

Saniyah sat speechless and gazed into Ryan's sincere eyes, trying to grasp the testimony she had just received. Her eyes glazed over, and she felt a single warm tear escape the corner of her eye and curve into the side of her mouth, followed by an uncontrollable flow. She took Ryan's face in her hands and brought him closer. She kissed his lips and moved her arms around him in a tight, loving embrace.

Between kisses Ryan found the time and air to ask, "Is that a yes?"

Saniyah replied by pulling his lips back to hers. Visions of a fairytale future occupied her mind as she kissed her Prince Charming. The intensity of the kiss and thoughts of realizing her happily ever after had Saniyah's poisoned apple throbbing. So she began to unbutton Ryan's shirt.

With no questions asked, he picked her up and wrapped her legs around his waist. She licked the side of his neck and ended her trail with a succulent kiss on his cheek. He removed her chef's coat and unbuttoned the blouse underneath. He wedged his hands between her bra and body and worked the garment up until her breasts hung free. He examined the perky twins with his tongue, assuring each one got equal attention.

Saniyah moaned with delight as his tongue ran marathons around her nipples. Her tone had Ryan ready for more, and he slipped his hand into her pants to prepare her for insertion. But a knock on the door interrupted his progress.

Knowing that the door was unlocked, they both hopped up and began to redress. When they were both decent, Ryan swung open the door to find, Chris, the 16-year-old dish washer.

"What you need, Chris?" Impatient intimidation was written all over Ryan's face as a signal for Chris to keep his visit brief.

"We…uh…need Miss Saniyah back in the kitchen…uh…Somebody dropped the dressing tray." Chris' confidence faded into an insecure stutter, and he looked away from his boss' scowl to regain his composure.

"Okay, I'll be right there." Saniyah tried to iron out the wrinkles in her chef coat with her hands and make one last improvement to her disheveled appearance.

Satisfied with her response, Chris nodded and disappeared into the kitchen. Before exiting, Saniyah turned back and said, "I probably won't see you again 'til closing time."

"It's all good, Roomie. We got plenty of time to spend together."

Reese returned to an empty table, which she slightly expected after leaving Andre's love declaration hanging. But instead of searching for her MIA man, she decided to go next door to Club Humidity and have a drink. She hoped the prolonged separation would weaken the flames of the argument she knew would be waiting when they reconnected.

Humidity's dance floor was packed as usual, but Reese had her sights set on the main bar that stretched the length of the nightclub's back wall. She made her way to a rare empty seat paying little attention to the numerous masculine eyes roaming over her existence. The hormone-fueled stares would have normally had her ego in full bloom, but they meant nothing that night. Thoughts of 'to love' or 'not to love' trumped their importance. Her face fell into her hands, and she plunged deeper into her dilemma of devotion until a vaguely familiar voice brought her up for air.

"Hey, don't I know you?"

Reese turned to match the face to the voice and was greeted with the unforgettable smile and chiseled frame of, Terrance, her recent on-the-job acquaintance. Her strong attraction to this man was immediately revived and began to build a sturdy frame of lust within her. That time around, thoughts of Andre struggled to hold top billing in her mind.

"No. I don't think so." Reese's lie veiled her desire.

"Yeah I do. You're the girl from the Oasis. Reese, right?" Terrance's name recognition caught Reese off guard. She was planning to create a new identity in an attempt to end the conversation. But his iron-clad memory ripped the legs off of that plan.

"That's me." Reese confirmed with an uncomfortable grin.

"You remember me? Terrance…the football player." Terrance's face pleaded once more for recognition.

"Oh yeah. How you doing?" Reese turned around to face him, and the full experience of his presence overwhelmed her. She could not ignore his perfect build and found herself sneaking glimpses below his neck. Her eyes were in sync with those of the numerous other women in the vicinity whose stares were much less obscure. Terrance was draped in a baggy, velour sweat suit, and on his feet were a fresh pair of white Air Force ones with black trim. His curly hair was gelled down to his scalp in twists, and his freshly-trimmed goatee framed his full, luscious lips. The scent radiating from his body was so clean and strong that Reese found herself trying to decipher what cologne he was wearing.

"I'm doing very well now that I see you, Sweetheart, but you look like you could use some attention." Terrance assumed. "What's wrong?"

"Nothing's wrong with me. I'm doing just fine." Reese's lie did not match her facial expression.

"Yeah, right." Terrance replied. "Let me buy you a drink, and you can tell me all about it. Okay?"

His kind tone and Reese's light wallet made her give in. "Fine. Buy me a drink and I'm all yours."

She regretted the submissive inference in her comment, but she did want to talk to someone about her issues -- someone besides Andre. She wanted an outside opinion, and Terrance seemed willing to really listen.

He ordered two Long Island iced teas, and the couple made their way to an empty table. They sat down and Reese began to pour all her problems out onto the table. Terrance listened to every word and was very attentive, which attracted Reese even more. His witty opinion on her situation, which mainly reflected on how much better of a match he was for her than Andre, helped to put Reese's troubled mind at ease. The laughter that came from the table made the pair appear more like old friends than two-time associates.

After a twenty minute conversation, Terrance looked at the time on his platinum Movado watch and decided to cut the night short. In the morning, he had an important business meeting about a potential endorsement deal with a local car dealership, and he wanted to be on his A-game for the owners. He pulled his Blackberry out of his sweat suit pocket.

"Can I give you my number?"

Without thought, Reese replied, "Yeah." She pulled out her iPhone, and the two proceeded to swap digits.

"Well, Miss Reese, I had a great time talking with you, but I'm gonna have to call it a night." Terrance wrapped. "Give me a call. I'm in town for a few days. Maybe we can hook up again."

"I will."

The two shared no more words but ended their meeting with a warm embrace, which allowed Reese to get more acquainted with Terrance's scent and the strong build hidden by his loose attire. While she melted in his arms, Terrance appreciated the softness of her chin rubbing against his neck, and the press of her supple breasts into his chest had him fighting the urge to invite her back to his hotel room.

Andre could not believe his own stupidity at revealing his true feelings to Reese so soon in their relationship. Her frazzled stare and excuse to exit the situation burned his memory like hot coals, a sensation he had become accustomed to from past relationships. He thought this time around would be different, although he couldn't think of one good reason why. With Reese's history, he should have known not to take it to the "L" word so soon, especially with it being his first time admitting it to himself.

The tension building inside him was too much to bear indoors so when Reese excused herself from the table, he went out to the patio to let the chilly, Gulf Coast breeze clear his mind. As he watched the murky, green waves rise and fall against the beach sands in the distance, he looked to the heavens for a solution to his problem. He thought.

"Where the Hell did this go wrong? What did I do? Why can't she just love me back, God?"

Out of nowhere, his spiritual meditation was interrupted by an infamous voice.

"Why you out here looking all depressed?" The voice was accompanied by a familiar scent and a soft touch on his shoulder. He turned to face, Latisha, his ex-girlfriend. She embraced him as if they had never parted ways. He hesitated to return the affection, but the familiarity of her grasp compelled him to put his arms around her waist. As she loosened the space between them, she planted a gentle kiss on Andre's cheek. He pulled back, not allowing it to go any further than a peck.

Latisha responded to his resistance, "Oh, it's like that now?"

"What you expect it to be like?"

"You still mad at me, Pookie?" Latisha said with fraudulently innocent doe eyes. Andre's disgusted scowl answered her question.

"Don't look at me like that."

"What you want, Tisha?"

"I miss you, Boo. Why you tripping?" Latisha's eyes begged for hope. "I let you have your little break to cool off. It's time for you to come back to Mama."

Andre's expression changed from disgust to surprise at her audacity. He knew he had to bring the imaginary relationship she thought they still had to an official close.

"We through, Girl. I moved on, and I'm sure you've already found plenty of men to fill in for me."

His unbending bluntness shrouded Latisha's face in shock. But it didn't take long for the fires of her vengeful wrath to flare.

"You damn right, Nigga. Mama ain't about to go hungry! Matter fact, I filled your position before you even quit!"

Her spew of hatred did not garner the response she was seeking. Andre merely smiled and shook his head at the revelation of facts he already knew. His need for air and his desire to carry on the conversation ended simultaneously. Latisha's verbal assault made him realize that he needed to make it work with Reese. She did all she could to uplift his spirit at all times, and he was not ready to give that feeling up just because her heart wasn't opening as fast as his.

As Andre turned his back on his past and began to walk towards the door to find his future, Latisha decided to make his journey a little rockier.

"I see that half-breed bitch got you wide open, huh?"

That time, her words stopped Andre in his tracks. She could say what she wanted about him, but he was not about to let her disrespect Reese.

"That *woman* is my woman now. And she takes way better care of me than you ever did."

"I'm sure she takes good care of you and every other nigga that got them legs open."

"Shut up. You don't know what you talking about, Trick." Andre yelled to drown out the truth in her words. His rage let Latisha know she had bruised his fragile ego. But a bruise did not satisfy her intent to break him so she continued to bash on his buttons.

"Nigga, you know that girl will drop her drawls for any man with fat pockets and good dick! Your dick is alright, but it ain't enough to make her forget you broke as Hell! How long you think she gonna keep your broke ass around before the next baller comes along?"

Latisha's tirade was like venom pumping through Andre's veins. His first thought was to put his hands around her neck and squeeze, but he was definitely not the man to engage in violence against any woman. She had backed him into a corner he didn't know how to escape.

Latisha leaned back with a victorious grin, admiring the look of defeat on her opponent's face. She was eating up the lost look in his eyes as he searched for a comeback to her insults. She was not about to let *her man* put any other woman up on a pedestal, especially one who didn't deserve it. If she had to be lonely, at least until the next victim came along, then she wanted him to be lonely, too. But the next words out of Andre's mouth ended her short-lived victory over his spirit.

"Reese may have lived a wild past, but she's dedicated to me now. I love her, and we gonna be together so I'd appreciate if you and your little stank ass attitude stay the fuck out of our lives!"

The finality of his declaration made Latisha understand that things were really over between them. She was willing to accept defeat after seeing the sincerity in his eyes. But she would not go down without one final blaze of glory. As Andre turned to walk away, she hurled one last insult that sent him back inside with just as much confusion as he had when he first came out.

"Don't come running back to me when that trick leave your ass."

Andre let Tisha's hurtful words bounce off his back. He pulled the door open to the vibrant restaurant atmosphere and abandoned his former lover. Though the prediction of her words had scared Andre, he was determined to make it work with the new lady in his life. He was confident that if he eased up on the LOVE gas and let Reese come around on her own terms, their relationship would remain strong.

Andre went back to his table to find that Reese had still not returned. He searched the restaurant and even had an unknown lady to look for Reese in the women's restroom. It didn't take long for him to realize she was no longer in the restaurant, and before he resorted to calling her phone, he decided to check the club.

Andre walked into Humidity and found Reese sitting at the bar with a gold-tooth wearing brother grinning in her face. Andre clenched his fist and was about to rush over in jealous-boyfriend mode when he noticed the apathetic look on Reese's face and the bent arm that was barely keeping her head from falling on the bar. His rage simmered and he walked toward the pair with a confident stride.

When he reached them, the gold-tooth grin faded into animosity as Reese's unnamed caller sized up his game's intruder. Reese perked up at the sight of Andre, and her face filled with relief that her knight in shining armor had come to rescue her from the unwanted advances of the bourbon-breathing dragon.

Andre addressed his unworthy opponent. "Excuse us, Player. I need to talk to my girl." His towering stature, masked loosely by his smile, was enough to let the 5-foot-7, 155-pound brother know a physical fight was out of the question.

"Oh, my bad, Bro. She didn't tell me she had a man."

"Yes, I did." Reese's interjection squashed his attempt to save face so he tucked his tail and made a quiet, abrupt exit. Reese and Andre shared a laugh once they were alone, but amusement was short-lived for Andre. He pulled Reese up from the bar stool and looked at her with intense eyes. She returned a nervous stare, remembering they had yet to discuss his failed love declaration.

"I want to apologize to you, Boo." Andre stated.

"Apologize? For what?"

"I shouldn't have pressed you by saying what I said. It's just too soon. I should have never...."

Reese interrupted, "I love you, too, Andre!"

They both wore the same astonished expression. Andre was shocked at how soon Reese had come around and, at the same time, wondered if her words were sincere or just her way of avoiding conflict. Reese, on the other hand, was shocked by her loose lips and wondered whether the Long Island iced tea had fueled her mouth's betrayal of her mind.

Since the words were already floating in the atmosphere, Reese knew she couldn't take them back. So she let her liquored-down expression of admiration stand, knowing her relationship would be better because of it. She craved the stability they had and refused to allow her issues to ruin another relationship.

Andre couldn't find the sincerity he sought in Reese's eyes, but he reacted as if he had. He embraced her tightly and followed with a sloppy, overzealous kiss that Reese normally would have detested. But the comfort she felt in his caring arms was enough to trump the lack-luster lip lock.

"So it took a Long Island Iced Tea for you to love me?" Andre laughed, but his confidence was less than amused. Reese knew his playful disposition was masking uncertainty, but she blurted a comedic response to veil her awareness.

"A buzzed mouth speaks a sober mind."

Chapter 7

Two weeks after the Boiling Point's eventful opening night, Ryan found himself about to make the biggest commitment to a woman he had ever made. His transition from player to live-in boyfriend perplexed him. He was shocked that he had even asked Saniyah to move in with him. And now he was overwhelmed by his eagerness to make it happen as soon as possible.

Ryan showed up to Saniyah's door at the crack of dawn on a Saturday morning. She and Reese were both sleeping when his spastic poke of the doorbell rang throughout the apartment. Reese's eyes popped open and she painfully sat up in bed. She slid on her Winnie the Pooh slippers before fumbling out of bed and into the living room.

"Do you know what time it is?" Reese snapped as soon as she opened the door. She looked up into Ryan's smiling face with half-opened, drowsy eyes and lifted her hand to her face to block the rising sunshine.

"Yeah…time to make this move." Ryan answered with little regard for Reese's hazy condition. Her droop turned into a scowl, and she went in search of Saniyah muttering about his indifference. Ryan came in the apartment and picked up one of the brown, cardboard boxes Saniyah had packed the previous night. Saniyah came into the living room with Reese following close behind.

"Hey, Baby." Saniyah yawned. "Why you here so early?"

"I'm ready to have you all to myself."

"Aww, my baby loves me." Saniyah crooned and planted a kiss on his cheek.

Ryan smiled. He put the box down and pulled Saniyah close to him. The two begin to exchange playful kisses.

"Excuse me." Reese coughed. "I don't wanna see all that."

"Well, close your eyes." Ryan countered.

"Sounds good to me." Reese said. "Good morning and good night."

At that, Reese made her way back to her bedroom and flopped down on her bed. The sheets were still warm from her body heat so she snuggled right back into her earlier position and quickly floated back to sleep.

Ryan and Saniyah continued their kissing session for a few more moments before Ryan cut it short and got back to business. Saniyah only had a few boxes to move so between the two of them, Ryan's car was fully loaded in no time.

Once they arrived at Ryan's apartment complex, the two were confronted with an unexpected hurdle. The elevator in the parking garage, the same one Ryan had just used a few hours ago, was once again out of order.

"I'm tired of this shit, man!" Ryan yelled. "Them stupid ass owners need to get off they ass and fix this thing!"

Out of his frustration with the building landlords, Ryan repeatedly kicked the elevator door and turned over the nearest trash can.

"Baby, calm down. It's no big deal." Saniyah reasoned. "We can take the stairs."

Ryan paused from his raging outburst long enough to see Saniyah's concerned expression. It was clear that his unnecessary anger bothered her. So he made the effort to calm down.

"You right." He conceded. "Sorry about that."

"It's cool." Saniyah walked over to him and gave him a reassuring embrace and peck on the lips. "Now let's get this over with."

The couple began the arduous task of carrying the boxes up the stairs to Ryan's second-floor apartment. And they flopped onto the couch after all of the boxes were in the apartment to take a quick breather before unpacking.

"I guess I better call Reese over to help me coordinate my things." Saniyah explained.

"Don't be thinking I'm gonna let y'all girly-up my spot 'cause I ain't." Ryan laughed with an all-powerful arrogance.

"I'm not trying to *girly-up* your spot." Saniyah corrected. "I'm trying to make *our* spot feel more comfortable."

"Well, just don't get too carried away with it." Ryan warned. "I can't be having *our* spot looking like the froo-froo room."

Saniyah pulled her cell phone out of her back pocket and called Reese. The phone rang five times and immediately went to voicemail.

While Saniyah left a message, Ryan started opening her boxes. His task was suddenly halted when he opened a box and found it full of Saniyah's underwear. His curiosity and male instinct would not let this go without some inspection. He started scrambling through the entire box examining each pair he picked up. And the panty raid would have continued until each one was analyzed if Saniyah had not interrupted.

"What do you think you're doing?" She confronted. She closed the box and snatched her under garments from Ryan's perverted clutches. He managed to steal one away, a lacy black pair, and held it up tauntingly. He started twirling it around his finger. Saniyah lunged at him, trying to rescue her distressed belongings. Instead, she lost her balance and toppled into him, knocking them both to the floor. She looked down into his laughing face and had the urge to kiss him so she quieted his humor with a gentle peck on the side of his face. Ryan gave her his full attention and the innocent kiss led to a tongue-twisting make-out session.

      Ryan stiffened with excitement and pulled his new roommate into him. He put his hands under her t-shirt and unhooked her bra. He cupped her breast in both hands as they continued to make out. His touch made Saniyah's waters flow and she started taking her clothes off piece by piece, flinging them to the floor, until she was completely naked. Seeing her undress added to Ryan's excitement and he quickly followed suit.

Saniyah mounted Ryan's manhood and immediately took charge. She rode him like she was trying to win the Kentucky Derby. And all Ryan could do was lay back with his eyes closed, mouth opened, and arms sprawled out across the floor.

Saniyah decided to switch things up and brought her romp to an abrupt halt. She got off of Ryan and started kissing his chest. The move confused him. He looked up to see what was going on.

"What you doing?"

"Hush." Saniyah's whisper was soft but demanding.

Ryan did as he was told and was quickly rewarded for his obedience. Saniyah moved her kissing trail down to Ryan's happy trail. She began to caress Ryan with her hand and then with her mouth.

"Wow!" Ryan thought as his bucked eyes watched Saniyah's head moving in and out. The treat was definitely unexpected from his usually passive lover. Her efficiency made him question how many times she'd gone there in the past, but her status as an amateur was established when he felt a painful scrape from her teeth. He almost screamed but held back in an effort to savor the moment.

When Saniyah's impromptu performance was over, Ryan returned the favor, and they both came to a climactic ending. Exhaustion soon set in, and they rested in each other's arms in the middle of the floor to recuperate.

Saniyah bragged. "Bet you gonna let me girly the spot up now, huh?"

Andre pulled his Mustang onto 33rd Avenue from Highway 90 around 11:30 a.m., passing between the banana-yellow frame of the Island View Casino and the iron-fenced floral landscape of Vrazel's Fine Food Restaurant. He made his way to the casino's employee parking lot, which sat to the rear of Vrazel's too-rich-for-his-pockets exterior.

His shift on the blackjack tables was set to start thirty minutes later, but he knew if he didn't get to work with time to spare, he would be late just roaming the isles of the jam-packed lot for an empty space. He found one only three rows back from the street, a rare occurrence, next to a rusty, tan 1985 Honda Civic. He snatched the vest that completed his uniform from the passenger seat and proceeded to engage in the multi-tasks of putting the vest on while exiting his vehicle.

Before making the short trip to the employee locker room, he stared directly across the street at the abrasively yellow and white-trimmed structure. The architecture of the casino -- which to Andre resembled a huge replica of the old, antebellum houses that lined the Coast prior to Hurricane Katrina's landing -- was stunning. He loved to admire the beauty of the building before making his way inside to its hectic, fortune-consumed atmosphere.

Andre entered the employee locker room and headed directly to his assigned locker, eager to put his Crescent City School of Gaming training to use another day. *32, 19, 55*, the numbers to his school-locker-turned-work-locker combination instinctively entered his brain.

Just as he was about to spin the dial on the lock to the first number, he saw his supervisor coming through and decided to stop and acknowledge him. But he soon realized that his boss was not just coming through but was headed in his direction with eyes aimed at him like darts. Andre immediately examined the demeanor of his approaching boss, searching for clues to his impending confrontation. His posture was stiff and his stride was definite. His right hand contained a single sheet of white copy paper with print Andre's perfect 20/20 vision was not strong enough to read.

Before Andre could decipher which of the many ideas floating in his head could be written on that paper, the boss man was on his side. His aimed and cocked eyes softened a bit once he reached his destination. He spoke cool and soft, as was his tone, but his words were definitely different from the conversations the two men normally shared.

"Can I speak to you for a moment, Mr. Sullivan?" He requested, trying his best to disguise his broken, Gulf Coast drawl with a proper, professional accent. The fact that his normally casual boss had called him by his last name took Andre by surprise.

"What's up, Kurt?" Andre replied. "I mean...Mr. Washington." Andre's second mind told him he should probably return the professional regard in this conversation. Kurt winced out a painful smile at Andre's exchange, revealing the wrinkles in his deep brown forehead and around his almond-colored eyes. His right hand fidgeted, causing the crinkle of the paper to interrupt the silence that hung between them.

"Well, Andre, I just got word from corporate that we're going to have to downsize our floor operations due to low numbers the last few quarters."

The sophisticated words of the 20-year tenured pit boss threw Andre for a loop, but the doom in their meaning was becoming painfully clear.

"If I didn't know any better, I'd think you was getting ready to let me go, Kurt."

Andre's eyes pleaded for relief from the fear of where he felt this conversation was headed. His boss's sorrow-filled expression did little to ease the tension that was building. And when Kurt dropped his face down to take in the black-and-white tiled floor instead of his likeable employee's pitiful gaze, Andre knew the situation was hopeless.

"You know if it was up to me, you'd be the last person to go. But what corporate wants has to be done. And they want you gone, Man." Kurt explained, making one last effort to comfort Andre while detaching himself from responsibility. He placed his hand on Andre's shoulder; his expression telling his ex-employee he was still a friend.

Andre gave his former boss an accepting glance before turning back to the combination lock on his former locker. His silence told Kurt their conversation was over so he handed Andre the walking paper and made a speedy exit from the somber situation.

When his boss was out of sight, Andre crushed the paper into his pants pocket and lifted his hand to the lock dial one last time.

He whispered through gritted teeth, "*32, 19, 55.*"

Chapter 8

Reese was sprawled out across the couch in the living room, staring blankly at the television in front of her. Although it displayed a rerun of her favorite TV show, *Girlfriends*, the images on the set were far from her mind. Her gaze soon shifted from the flickering flat screen to find the source of the chirps she was hearing. Her focus soon settled on a Blue Jay perched on a branch of the magnolia tree recently planted in front of the living room window. But just as her eyes were becoming familiar with the bird's sky Blue complexion, it thrust itself into the air and vanished. Reese thought.

"Damn! Even the wildlife is abandoning me."

She was fed up with the sudden onset of loneliness upon her life. Not only had Saniyah practically forgotten she existed after shacking up with Ryan, but her own man had also deserted her after being laid off from his job to visit and solicit his successful, but estranged architect father in Jackson.

Reese's first thought to cure her isolation was to call a female associate and make plans to hit either a club, bar, strip joint, casino – or all of the above according to how the night played out. But her second mind reminded her that she was no longer on speaking terms with the few females she *used* to hang with, most of them having fallen out with her because of her tendency to catch too firm a grasp on their boyfriends' attention. The others simply avoided her once they found a man they intended to keep.

With one solution to her solitary confinement going down in flames, her mind wondered to another fragile issue in her life. Since uttering the "L" word to her more-devoted-thanthou boyfriend, she had been questioning whether she really expected their relationship to last.

Though she begged God to give her the feelings for Andre she knew he had for her, their lack of formation was sending her strong signals that it might not be what God wanted for her, the universe was sending a completely different message from what she thought. Andre's lack of employment was also an issue that was hard for Reese to overlook. She could not remember the last time she was with a man that was not gainfully employed -- or at least illegally gainful. And the possibility that she could end up with a man who would not be able to provide the lifestyle with which she was accustomed sent chills up and down her spoiled spine. Andre was sexy as a blackjack dealer with potential to become management, but as an out of work, too-pretty-for-tugging bum, he was getting less attractive by the day.

Reese was drowning in negativity when the buzz, and subsequent ring, of her cell phone against her thigh pulled her from the depths of despair. She pulled the expensive gadget from the squeeze of her jeans pocket. Terrance's name showed up on the display. Her hesitation allowed for a few more seconds of Salt and Pepa's classic "I'll Take Yo' Man" to blast from the speaker on her phone. But quick reflection on the loneliness of her situation, influenced her finger to press accept.

"Hello."

"Hey, Girl. How you doing?" Terrance's sexy baritone oozed through the receiver and trickled down between Reese's thighs, causing her to make an airy reply she regretted.

"I'm good." She regained her control. "What you doing calling me?"

"I'm *calling you* because I'm in town, and I wanted to know if you wanted to hang out."

"You do realize I have a man that might not be too comfortable with that, right?"

"I know…. I just want to see you." Terrance changed his approach. "Maybe we can all hang out. You think he'd be cool with that?"

"I don't know and can't find out 'cause he's out of town."

Reese could not understand why she was divulging all of that information, especially to her temptation of the month.

"Well, if he's out of town, I'm sure he won't have a problem with me taking you out." Terrance responded just as Reese expected.

"How you know he won't mind?" Reese questioned.

"Because he can't mind what he doesn't know."

He had Reese trapped in a lust-filled corner. Andre and the sex had been absent for a week now. And the addict in Reese, which Terrance had managed to arouse with his voice alone, was craving the next hit. She could not even fathom spending another night - especially a Friday night - alone. So before the angel of fidelity could land on her shoulder, she was ready to accept a night with her new found *friend*.

"Okay. You got me for the night." Reese conceded.

"Cool. I was thinking we could go to this Cirque du Soleil thing that's going on at the hotel where I'm staying."

Reese could tell by his tone that his suggestion was merely an attempt to gauge her interests. And she wasn't really feeling the whole acrobatic theatrics thing either so she made a counter offer better suited to entertain them both.

"Why don't we just go get a drink?"

"Sounds good." Terrance exhaled relief. "As a matter of fact, I got a room at the Beau Rivage. Why don't you meet me in the casino lounge around 10?"

"Okay...see you then."

Reese pulled up to the front entrance of the Beau Rivage Hotel and Casino. Before she could reach for the car door handle, a pimple-faced, teenaged parking attendant was yanking the door open and offering a helping hand to assist her exit out of the vehicle. She regally accepted the offer of assistance from the attendant, who considered the view of her swaying curves as she entered the casino to be an added bonus to his anticipated tip.

Once inside, Reese made her way to the Eight75 lounge and immediately spotted Terrance waiting for her at the bar. She sashayed over to him. Every man she passed took notice of the light-skinned sister draped in a form-fitting, coal grey knit top with the draped cowl neckline exposing her buttermilk shoulders, a pair of black, poured on leggings, and four-inch silver stiletto pumps. Terrance also took notice and took another sip of his Corona to postpone his launch.

"You look good, Girl!" He said as he stood up to pull out an empty barstool for his companion.

"So do you." She replied, searching for the fill of his muscles through his short-sleeve, khaki button up and fitted dark blue denim jeans. She sat down on her stool, and Terrance followed suit, his pearly whites and grey gaze still twinkling in the darkness of the lounge.

"So what you drinking?" Terrance asked.

"I think I'm feeling vodka and Red Bull tonight." Reese answered, looking at him with a devilish smirk.

"You sure you can handle that?" He continued, neither refusing to break their gaze upon one another.

"Trust me." Reese bragged. "I can handle anything."

Before turning to the bartender to put in their requests, Terrance got in the last words.

"I think I need to find that out for myself."

The baritone over the phone was not nearly as potent as it was in person. Reese had to clinch her crossed legs tight to hide the trembling and was relieved when her drink was finally delivered. She took a long, slow sip from the straw, allowing the energized intoxication to trickle down her throat and drown her inhibitions. Her slow sip captured Terrance in a trance as he watched her full, glossy lips work the unsuspecting straw.

When their cocktail glass and beer bottle were empty, Reese had an ounce more courage and spunk inside. She stood up from the bar and walked over to Terrance, forcing her body between his slightly opened legs. She leaned into him and whispered in his ear.

"You wanna dance?"

Terrance answered her question by standing up and motioning for her to lead the way. The lounge didn't have much room for dancing, but most of the other loungers were busy drinking and talking so the couple was able to find a spot. The sound system belted out the smooth sounds of a Jazz band.

Neither Reese nor Terrance was really accustomed to Jazz, but they made it work. Reese pulled Terrance's embrace in from behind, winding and grinding against his groin. She felt his rock getting harder and harder. He leaned over and gently sucked on her neck. Reese felt her secrets sweating and knew her body was ready to go there. She turned around and pulled Terrance's shirt toward her until their lips met, and they engaged in a liquor-laced lip lock.

After the kiss, Reese pulled Terrance's ear to her now-glossless mouth and whispered.

"Can I see your room?"

Without any more words, Terrance retreated to the bar to close out his tab. When he returned to Reese, he grabbed her hand and swiftly, but carefully maneuvered her out of the lounge, through the maze of people entering and leaving the casino and to the hotel elevator. He pushed the up button, without releasing her hand.

When the elevator doors opened, the couple entered the empty chariot side by side. The doors closed, and the lip lock commenced again until the doors reopened on the eighth floor. The couple, still hand in hand, made their way to room 812. Terrance's impatient hands made unlocking the door more of a task than it should have been, taking four unsuccessful swipes of his key card before he finally got it right.

Once inside the hotel room, Reese excused herself to the bathroom. Terrance took her absence as his opportunity to set the mood. First, he pulled down the covers on the king-sized bed. Then, he turned the clock radio to the first slow jam he could find --"At Your Best" by Aaliyah. Finally, he stripped down to his black boxer briefs, which clung tightly to his swollen, steroid-free package, and pulled back the long lace curtains hanging over the glass balcony doors to reveal the dark, moonlight-speckled Gulf Coast waters below.

    Just as Terrance was about to pour himself a shot of Hennessy, Reese exited the bathroom wearing nothing but her silver stilettos. He almost dropped the bottle in his hands but regained his composure and put it back in its place unharmed. Reese's sexy stalk seduced him as she made her way over to where he was standing. She put her arms around his neck and examined every part of his mouth with her Kailua-flavored gloss-covered lips. Terrance gently cupped her bare cheeks and lifted her legs around his waist. The couple continued to kiss as he carried her over to the exposed glass doors and let her stilettos return to the floor. He leaned into her ear and whispered.

"Turn around."

Reese did as she was told. She spotted a few floating boats beyond the balcony and immediately thought about the possibility of someone catching their open show, especially on film. She imagined Andre watching "Cowboys Running Back Caught Sexing Random Chick" on YouTube and almost panicked. But before she could protest their position, Terrance's full-grown stroke penetrated her from behind and made everything else irrelevant. The impact of his thrust was too much for her to handle alone and she was forced to press her body against the cold, hard glass doors for support.

Terrance worked her from behind and brought a sweet, innocent moan out of her that she had never made with any other man. Andre's stroke could normally lower the volume on her aggressive, shit-talking. But Terrance had managed to reduce it to an almost silent 'purr' for the mercy that she did not really want. So it wasn't long before her ride on the Terrance Express had erased all thoughts of anything Andre.

Terrance's slow, deliberate pound became a fast, reckless pump as he got closer to his peak. Every thrust caused Reese's stiletto heels to jerk slightly off the floor. The fullness of his entry caused her to squirm and reach back in an effort to push him away and signal him to slow down. Terrance responded to Reese's attempt at relief by holding her arms down and whispering into her ear.

"Don't run. *Handle it*, Girl," mocking the bold statement she had previously made. Reese accepted his challenge. She dug her forehead into the glass door, bit her bottom lip, and took her pleasurable punishment.

Terrance appreciated Reese's effort, but he was determined to dominate her and leave no question about who was in control. He reduced his pump to an agonizingly blissful slither that brought tears to his conquest's eyes and caused a long, uncontainable groan of climax to escape her tight-lipped mouth. Her display of joy and pain influenced him to make an eruption of his own that flowed from his body to hers and ended in shivers that nearly paralyzed them both.

Terrance fell back into the nearest chair and exhaled satisfaction. Reese, still processing what had been done to her, remained stoic up against the glass. The fog from her panting mouth was the only part of her that moved until her body realized it was free to work on its own again. She slid down to the floor, leaving a trail of sweat on the glass door.

After a few moments, Terrance looked down from his state of tranquility long enough to see Reese's tired, naked frame still pressed up against the glass door in a sex-induced stupor. Instead of risking waking her up by carrying her to the bed, he just took the goose down comforter off the bed, joined her on the floor, and wrapped them both up inside the warmth of the spread. His kiss to her cheek was acknowledged by her semi-conscious mumble.

"Still undefeated."

December

Chapter 9

"Taylor for the win!" Ryan announced as he tossed a crumpled ball of tissue into the wastebasket by the door in his master bathroom. He mimicked the sounds of a thousand cheering fans and raised his arms to receive the fabricated praise as he witnessed the success of his effort. He then stood in the mirror, wearing nothing more than a pair of black basketball shorts and white low-cut socks, admiring the reflection of his thin, chiseled torso.

After a few moments of self-appreciation, he managed to slip into his black jersey and black and red Air Jordans. Saniyah walked into the bathroom in time to witness him complete his athletic ensemble by placing a black sweatband, with a red Jordan logo emblazoned on the front, around his wave-riddled fade. He decided to cut off his braids in order to better reflect the businessman he was becoming.

"Where you think you going?" Saniyah snapped.

"Me and Dre gonna play ball with some of our homeboys."

The smile Saniyah had been wearing deteriorated into a scowl at his unexpected revelation. She placed both hands on her hips and shifted her weight to one side.

"What's wrong with you?" He asked as he picked up his backpack and placed it on one shoulder.

"I thought you were spending the day with me."

Ryan had become so consumed by his dual roles managing the restaurant at dinner time and the club after hours, that the only time he had to himself was during the morning and afternoon. But even that time had been almost completely concentrated on Saniyah, and it was apparent to him that she was becoming accustomed to this arrangement. He enjoyed the time they spent together, but he also enjoyed freedom and did not appreciate her attempt to control him.

"I can't today, Boo." He explained. "I already told them I was gonna play. We can hang out tomorrow."

"But I bought tickets for us to go to the international food festival today. It only happens once every December."

"Well, we'll just have to catch it next time."

"Ryan!" She huffed. "These tickets were expensive *and* nonrefundable."

She pulled the tickets out of her jeans pocket and forced them into his hand. He examined their small print and verified that the festival was a "one day only" event. He shrugged his shoulders and gave Saniyah an unmoved stare before tossing the flimsy tickets onto the bathroom counter.

"I'm going to play ball." He proclaimed as he turned to exit the bathroom. "So I'll just have to make this up to you later."

"So, your boys are more important than me?"

The words stopped Ryan dead in his tracks. He knew he would have a fight on his hands if he did not handle the situation with care. He turned to face the frown of his prosecutor, brainstorming for an appropriate response.

"Of course not, Boo. But I've been spending time with you all week. I just want to hang with the fellas."

Ryan walked toward Saniyah in an attempt to console her that was immediately shot down when she backed away and folded her arms.

"The last time I checked, you were in a relationship with me." Saniyah snapped. "Or are you fucking your homeboys, too!"

The tone in her response was so laced with venom that it shocked her even more than her besieged boyfriend. But after the initial shock of her comment wore off, Ryan was filled with rage. He lunged at Saniyah and slammed her body against the bathroom wall, both hands holding a firm grasp on her crumpled T-shirt. She cried out as her body shriveled from the heat of his crazed stare.

"What you say?" He barked. Saniyah's only response was the fearful pant she made as tears welled up in her eyes and rolled down her cheeks.

"Yeah, you quiet now, huh?" He teased. He put one hand around her jaw and upper neck and forced her to look up at him. He looked into her watery eyes and leaned in close enough to feel the warmth of the rapid breaths from her panicked pant against his chin.

"Don't you ever say some shit like that to me." Ryan demanded. "I am a man, and I'm tired of you trying to run me like some little boy."

Saniyah took in every word in silence, praying her cooperation would bring a speedy end to the altercation. To her relief, his satisfaction with her surrender eased his grasp and lightened his tone.

"Now, I'm going to play ball with my boys, and I'll see you at the restaurant later. Okay?"

Saniyah managed to shake her constrained head in agreement. The continued cooperation of his captive pleased Ryan, and he shoved Saniyah out of his clutches, forcing her to bump into and knock over the wastebasket. Its contents spilled onto the floor as Saniyah struggled to regain her footing and avoid falling, prompting Ryan to make a final command to his bewildered lover before making a triumphant exit from the room.

"Clean that shit up before you leave, too."

Reese sat in the lobby of her gynecologist's office, awaiting her turn under the microscope. For the past two months, she had suffered from spells of nausea and irritability -- including her Thanksgiving night spent hugging the toilet after attacking Saniyah's holiday feast -- with no trace of a period. She waited two months to make the appointment out of faint hope that her M.I.A. crimson friend would return, but when late October and November passed without so much as a spot, she knew it was time to face the music. Although she hated to spend her $20 co-pay just for her doctor to state the obvious, the skeptic in her needed professional confirmation.

Reese flipped through the pages of the doctor's office copy of People Magazine while she waited for her name to be called. She didn't really concentrate on the content, with the distraction of her impending doom, but she couldn't help but be annoyed by the smiling faces of care-free celebrities and models that seemed to mock her situation. She flipped through to the back cover and realized she hadn't gained anything from the magazine's infotainment-filled pages except the strong urge to vomit from the smell of its perfume samples. She made a quick retreat to the lobby bathroom to relieve her stomach of the small lunch she had barely managed to hold down before arriving.

Reese looked at her watery eyes and drooled-stained chin in the bathroom mirror. She pondered her decision to share multiple unprotected sexual episodes with not one, but two men in the last few months, one of whom lived in an entirely different region of the country.

"How did I let this happen?"

In retrospect, she reasoned that the heat of the romantic moments she spent with both men would have fizzled at the suggestion that a pleasure-blocking condom be used. But she realized the consequence would last 17 years, 364 days and 23 hours longer than her raw romps in Dre and Terrance land.

Reese cleaned her face and returned to the lobby as a frustrated physician's assistant repeated her name to the unresponsive handful of women waiting for their own names to be called.

"I'm Reese." She said as she made her way toward the annoyed assistant.

"Dr. Montgomery will see you now. Follow me." She announced and turned to make her way down the narrow corridor. Reese followed her to an examination room where she checked vitals and weight, which was three pounds heavier than Reese was accustomed to. The assistant interrogated Reese about the reason for her visit, made some notes on her clipboard, and directed Reese to the examination room's small bathroom for a urine sample. Reese returned with a less than stellar, but good enough for testing specimen, and the assistant made her exit with the assurance that the doctor would be in shortly with the results.

The assistant's declaration made Reese cringe. She knew the condemnation of her actions from Dr. Montgomery, who had been her gynecologist since she first moved to Gulfport, would be brutal. He had become like a father figure to Reese over their three-year relationship of checkups, and he had already warned Reese about her sexually-deviant behavior after her last pregnancy scare turned out to be negative.

Dr. Montgomery walked into the room, 20 minutes after the assistant's exit, wearing a disappointed expression. He focused his frustrated gaze upon his patient, who responded by hanging her head in shame.

"Didn't I tell you not to bring yourself in here with this pregnancy mess again until after I attended your wedding, Miss Thang?" He lectured in the less than professional tone he reserved for Reese. She responded with a reluctant nod before looking up at her doctor with a pathetic pout.

"Don't give me that look, Young Lady. You won't get any sympathy from me this time. I tried to warn you the last time we went through this. Now, I just have one question for you."

"What?" Reese murmured through her slowly choking throat.

"Who's the baby's daddy?" The reality of his comment caught her off guard. It confirmed her pregnancy and the sad fact that she didn't know who was responsible. Telling Dr. Montgomery of her uncertainty would result in the continuation of his berating sermon so she told him what she hoped was true.

"My boyfriend, Andre, is the father."

"Is he a good guy?" Dr. Montgomery had only met one of Reese's past boyfriends when he bumped into them at a movie theater, and his beautiful client's surprisingly unattractive suitor looked less than upstanding.

"Yes, Dr. M. He's a really good guy, actually." She half stated, half reflected. Her statement was a precursor to contemplative thoughts on how she would tell her perfect boyfriend about her sexual faults. Her eyes watered at the thought of the hurt her revelations were bound to cause.

Dr. Montgomery saw the emotional disposition on her face and hoped she wasn't being dishonest with him about the character of her sperm donor. And before continuing with his examination to discern the specifics of her journey to motherhood, he ended the conversation with a comment he hoped would provide his bewildered patient with some clarity and guidance on her situation.

"I really hope so, Reese. But whether this guy stays in the picture or not, that baby is a permanent part of *your* life now. And from this point on, you're making decisions for two."

Selena Brooks Bio

Selena Brooks was born in 1984 on the Mississippi Gulf Coast, made in Pass Christian and raised in Gulfport. She graduated from Gulfport High School in 2002 and went on to earn a Bachelor's Degree in Communication from the University of South Alabama and a Master's Degree in Business Administration from Strayer University. She currently serves the Federal Government in a civilian capacity as an employee of the Department of Defense, as she has done for the past nine years. As a Mississippi native, she is well aware of the negative perceptions and ill-informed commentary at mere mention of the land lost between Louisiana and Alabama, and her goal as a writer is to give a realistic description of the Mississippi experience and its residents through the underexposed positive voice of the African

American community that characterized her own Creole heritage and upbringing on the Gulf Coast.

Made in the USA
Columbia, SC
04 November 2022